DAUGHTERS *of the* SEA

Lucy

KATHRYN LASKY

DAUGHTERS *of the* SEA

Lucy

SCHOLASTIC PRESS / NEW YORK

Library of Congress Cataloging-in-Publication Data Available

ISBN 978-0-439-78312-5

10 9 8 7 6 5 4 3 2 1   12 13 14 15 16

Printed in the U.S.A.   23
First edition, March 2012

The text type was set in ITC Cheltenham Book.
Book design by Lillie Howard

Searching my heart for its true sorrow
This is the thing I find to be:
That I am weary of words and people,
Sick of the city, wanting the sea;

Wanting the sticky, salty sweetness
Of the strong wind and shattered spray;
Wanting the loud sound and the soft sound
Of the big surf that breaks all day.

— Edna St. Vincent Millay

PROLOGUE

WASHINGTON SQUARE, NEW YORK CITY, 1899

MARJORIE SNOW, wife of the Reverend Stephen Snow, peered into the bedroom of her daughter, Lucy. In a corner on a table was the dollhouse that Aunt Prissy had given Lucy for her ninth birthday — a perfect replica of Prissy's estate, White Oaks. What a lovely house it had been, complete with the most charming decorations; even the wallpaper had been scaled down to dollhouse dimensions. And what had that peculiar little girl done but painted over it! A seascape, of all things. Not that she had made a mess of it. Hardly. Lucy had always exhibited an artistic bent far beyond her years. It was a lovely scene. But when Aunt Prissy came to visit, Marjorie could see that she was upset by the alterations to the house. She tried to cover her agitation by murmuring soft little exclamations, the verbal equivalent of the weak tea one might serve a patient convalescing from a stomach ailment.

"My . . . my . . . what changes you have made. Yes, you have quite an eye for detail. . . . And what happened to the French-style armoire? Oh, yes, there it is. You've painted it, too, I see. Sea anemones. And who might live here, Lucy? A nice little family, I imagine."

And then a most peculiar conversation ensued, much to Marjorie's consternation.

"Yes, Aunt Prissy. The Begats," Lucy answered softly, and a slight blush crept across her cheeks.

"The who? The Beggars?"

"No, the Begats. B-e-g-a-t-s." Lucy spelled the word out.

Her aunt Prissy complimented her on her spelling, then commented, "That's quite interesting, Lucy dear. Now, where did you ever come up with that name?"

Lucy's green eyes widened. "The Bible, Matthew, chapter one, verse one through seventeen."

"Oh, *those* Begats," Aunt Prissy exclaimed as if it were a distinguished family that she had somehow overlooked. "How very curious!"

"Well, her father is a minister, Priscilla," Marjorie interjected. "She does know the Bible. Only normal."

"Yes, of course. That must explain it."

The word *must* suggested that it had better explain it because Priscilla Bancroft Devries felt there was precious little else normal about this child.

Despite her peculiarities, Lucy was an obedient child. However, if there was one thing that Marjorie wished she could change, it was her daughter's tendency toward withdrawal. And of course the limp caused by her slightly turned foot. "Not a clubfoot," her mother was quick to assure everyone when they saw the infant for the first time. "Doctor Webb says it's ever so slight, and with the proper shoes, it is entirely correctable."

Lucy of course hated the proper shoes. She complained about them constantly and, when she was at home, would often scamper about in her stocking feet. The limp had decreased, but it had not disappeared entirely, and Marjorie felt that this was what inhibited her daughter in society. She disliked dancing for, she said, the shoes made her clumsy. And she would often stay rooted to one spot at a party, preferably behind the foliage of a large potted palm, rather than mingle with the guests. Lucy definitely was not a "mingler." In Marjorie Snow's mind, mingling was somewhere between an art form and a kind of elegant athleticism. She praised an aptitude for mingling as one might revere a good circulatory system. Marjorie hoped that Lucy would outgrow her shyness, but as she entered her teens, Lucy only blossomed into a wallflower.

This was most evident at the tea dances given at the Excelsior Gardens on Park Avenue. The Excelsior was a private club to which the Snows did not belong but were frequently invited, owing to the reverend's position as minister of St. Luke's.

With the possible exception of Trinity on Fifth Avenue, there was not a finer church than St. Luke's, which had produced two of the last three Episcopal bishops of the diocese of New York. And if Marjorie had her way, Stephen would succeed that doddering old fool who was the present bishop. That was when the Snows would truly get their due, part of which would include becoming members of the Excelsior Club. Stephen had promised. *"The office demands it,"* he had said. One simply could not become the bishop of New York without being invited to join the leading clubs. And the office would also demand that Lucy, dear Lucy, become a bit more outgoing.

Outgoing was a favorite word of Marjorie Snow's. Her recurring plea to Lucy was that she try a bit harder in "the social department" or sometimes "social area."

At least she had convinced Lucy to go to the afternoon reception the Ogmonts were giving for their niece, who had just arrived from Paris. The Ogmonts, who perched on the loftiest pinnacle of New York society, were related to the Drexels, and this was a coveted invitation for the young set. A last dip into society until people scattered to the summer watering holes in a few weeks.

And now the reverend had come home with wonderful news that they, too, would be joining the summer migration, and Marjorie had no one to tell it

to. She could write Prissy, of course, or possibly tele-
gram her, but that cost. They had a telephone, thanks
to the church, but Marjorie had no idea how to make
a long-distance call all the way to Baltimore. Oh, she
wanted to tell somebody! If only Lucy knew that her
father had been asked to be the summer minister in
Bar Harbor, Maine, she would have had so much to
talk about at the reception.

SPIRITS REVEALED

THROUGH THE FRONDS of the voluminous potted palm in the Ogmonts' Fifth Avenue apartment, Lucy Snow saw young Elsie Ogmont heading toward her with the Ogmont cousin Lenora Drexel, her brother Eldon Drexel, and his fiancée, Denise De Becque.

The three women were all very elegantly dressed in the latest fashion, Lenora in particular. Denise was the least attractive but had a great deal of style. She was wearing a blue watered-silk gown trimmed in ivory silk at the cuffs and neckline. As they came closer, Lucy wondered if it was perhaps Denise's expression, more than anything, that made her unattractive. She always looked vexed, a scowl of disapproval that bordered on outright contempt.

What if they come this way? What will I say? Lucy desperately tried to conjure up suitable topics for discussion, but her mind drew a blank. Luckily, Elsie spoke first.

"Lucy, I want to introduce you to Lenora. Of course, you already know her brother Eldon."

"Hello." Lucy extended her hand. "It has been a while."

"Yes," Lenora said. "I went to Paris almost three years ago." Lucy became acutely aware of how dull her gray faille tea gown must look next to Lenora's silk confection.

"But I have been a full-time Yankee," Eldon Drexel said. "And I have rarely seen you out. No excuse, Miss Snow. We need to see more of you, my dear, and not just in church." This evoked gay laughter from the three women, which made Lucy squirm.

She couldn't tell whether Eldon was mocking her or being sincere. In this strangely complex world, one had to speak but not actually say anything of substance. This was a world that rewarded glibness and sly wit and most often left her a-stutter.

"Did you not wish to see Paris, Mr. Drexel?"

"Some of us have to stay home and work, mind the coffers, so to speak."

So to speak? Lucy wondered if such a metaphor worked despite the fact that the Drexels owned banks. The coffers were real. Lucy noticed that when Denise's fiancé said the word *coffers*, her left eyebrow hiked up just slightly into the vast plains of her broad forehead. Her family, too, were bankers, and Lucy wondered if Denise somehow wanted credit for the healthy state of the Drexel coffers. This had been considered the engagement of the season — two old families with two old banks. A match made by Mammon!

Elsie seemed to pick up on Denise's disquiet and made a quick course correction in the conversation.

"Isn't Lenora's dress the most exquisite? The overlay of lace looks almost like a fine mist."

"Charles Worth," Lenora replied airily, as if wearing a five-hundred-dollar dress were as common an occurrence as brushing one's hair.

"Oh, yes, I've heard of him," Lucy said. The three young women exchanged slightly withering glances.

Lucy realized immediately the stupidity of what she had just said. Everyone had heard of Charles Worth, the most famous of Parisian designers.

Suddenly, it seemed very warm in the room. Her foot had begun to hurt. Probably from standing in one place. She knew she should mingle, as her mother would suggest. But with whom? Lucy knew she had been invited only out of deference to her father. She was sure the other guests had little interest in making conversation with a girl whose bloodlines were short and who had no prospects for an inheritance, not to mention her terribly outdated dresses.

The three ladies had begun to move away although Eldon lingered.

"Well . . ." Lucy was eager to move away before she made another blunder, but she did not know how to disentangle herself. Should she talk about banking? He must be good with figures and accounting. Perhaps she could ask him that. *Are you good with figures?* Lord, how vapid did that sound!

"Well?" Eldon Drexel cocked his head slightly and looked at her inquiringly. There was a light in his eye that she found disturbing.

"You must get very tired as a banker. I imagine it must be hard work looking at all those tiny figures all day long." He looked momentarily confused. "Gives you a headache, I suppose."

He threw back his head and laughed. It was a horrible, sneering sound. "Ah! Now I catch your drift. What a queer little creature you are. Surely, dear girl, you don't suppose we have to do that ourselves. We have people who do that. You know, the men with the green eyeshades."

Immediately, Lucy realized her mistake. Of course they had people like that. All the people in this room had people like that to take care of the small monotonies of life, to do everything. She was just thankful that her mother had not heard this exchange. She would have been mortified.

"I must really be going. I have an appointment." The color rose in her face. She blinked several times and tried to look over his shoulder as if something had caught her attention on the other side of the room.

"The church keeps you busy, I suppose, being a reverend's daughter and all." Then he tipped his head again to one side and looked at her in a way that made her feel quite uncomfortable. "I suppose that's what makes you so" — he paused as his eyes flitted down her gown — "refreshing." She caught sight of Denise glaring at both of them. There was no question about Denise De Becque's expression. She was livid.

"Yes, very busy," Lucy said abruptly. "Excuse me."

Two minutes later, she stepped out the front door onto the street. She knew she should have thanked her hosts, but she simply had to get out. Lucy breathed in great drafts of fresh air, but as she exhaled, all she felt was guilt. What would her mother say? Why couldn't she be like the other girls at the party? Eldon Drexel was dreadful, but there must be other young men who were nice, even if they were all rather boring. But maybe after the first flurry of love, marriage became boring. Then she stopped abruptly mid-thought. Was she even looking for marriage? What kind of life could there be without marriage? None, she supposed, but perhaps something in between where she was now and the inexorable future that was expected for her by her parents, by society, by everyone in Western civilization.

She certainly did not want to go home in this state and face her mother's inevitable questions about who was there and what they wore and how Lenora Drexel was after her "finishing off" in Paris. That was what her mother had called those three years, "Lenora's finishing off." It conjured up all sorts of peculiar images in Lucy's mind, from putting the final varnish on a painting to sewing the eyelids shut on a corpse and then adding a touch of rouge to the cheeks so the dead might be presentable, appear "healthy" while dead as a doornail. Her mother often talked about how nice So-and-So looked after attending a parishioner's funeral, always extolling the services of the Edwards and Beecham funeral parlor. "They deal only with the top drawer." "Top drawer" was one of her mother's many expressions for describing the celebrated upper echelons of New York society, alive or dead.

Slightly renewed by being outdoors, Lucy walked several blocks west, then caught a trolley up to the Museum of Natural History. With its miles of corridors and capacious galleries, the museum felt like an oasis from all the city's hubbub, the crowds and commotion, the clanging trolleys and barking street vendors.

Lucy knew some might think it odd that she could find solace among so many dead things — the skeletons of dinosaurs, along with other long-dead animals, preserved by whatever was the taxidermy equivalent to Edwards and Beecham. But something about the museum put her at ease, particularly the exhibits devoted to exotic cultures, their artifacts, and their ways of life.

Lucy wound her way through the natural history gallery to a new exhibit entitled Above the Circle: Spirits Revealed and began walking through the dim light of the vast gallery dedicated to Arctic culture. On the other side of the hall, a man was standing in front of a large case, addressing an audience.

"The Indians of the Arctic, the Inuit, were bound culturally by the regions of Canada as well as Alaska to the extreme west. I am here to talk to you today about an Inuit word. That word is '*Inua.*' *Inua* best translates into the word 'soul' or 'spirit.'" Lucy glanced at the figures inside the case. Even the frozen statues had more spirit than Eldon Drexel or anyone else at the Ogmonts' reception.

"From the paddles for their kayaks, or *umiaks*, as they called their sealskin boats, to the beading on their boots, the objects reveal the spirits that guided their every action."

A woman raised her hand. "Pardon me, Doctor Forsythe, but among these tribes, how were fishing boundaries established?"

"Madam, you make a common error. There were no tribes among the Inuit. The word '*tribe*' designates a political unit rather than a cultural one. The Inuit population was small, and the people were spread out too far over the vastness of the Arctic, to be organized into tribes like the Indians of our country and to have to concern themselves with boundaries."

"Oh, I see," the woman replied softly.

Lucy pressed closer to the front of the group. She now had a clear view of the small sealskin boat. In it sat a mannequin of an Inuit bundled in a sealskin parka with a hood trimmed in fur. A harpoon had been set in his hand. Museum artists had sculpted "ice" floes about him, and he appeared to glide across a painted sea. In the background was a twilit sky with stars just rising. It was a beautiful seascape. One that Lucy had never quite imagined. The lighting in the museum gave the sky a luminous greenish tinge. It almost made her chilly to look at it. So opposite to what she had felt less than an hour before as she stood near the potted palm.

And what would our objects reveal of our inua? Lucy mused as she thought about the party she had just left. The sparkling chandelier under which Eldon Drexel had informed her that he did not wear a green eyeshade and never touched the figure ledgers. She imagined a museum some time in the far distant future where the artifacts of Ogmonts and Drexels and the like might be displayed. For were they not a tribe, with their Charles Worth dresses, their Harvard or Yale signet rings? There could be two display cases really — one for the masters' artifacts and one for the servants with the starched black dresses and snowy aprons and, of course, the green eye-shades of the clerks. But of course the Inuit on their icebound outposts at the edge of the sea most likely did not have servants. There was no time for such class distinctions, she thought, as she looked long-ingly at the figure in the boat gliding across the painted sea.

Dr. Forsythe was answering a man who had asked a question about Inuit trade. "He is most likely hunt-ing the bearded seal down the coast a bit. What I mean by easy commerce is that the spirit life for the Inuit was as alive and vital as their temporal life. The borders between these two worlds were easily traversed, crossed over."

"Did they only fish in the summer?" someone else asked.

"Really, there were two basic seasons for the Inuit — Ice and No Ice. They went in their boats when the ice was clear or nearly clear. And when it wasn't, they went in their sleds and found the blow-holes for seals or walrus."

Lucy was mesmerized by the model maker's replica of the sea. She raised her hand shyly. "Did they ever cross the sea in those boats?"

"Ah, a very interesting question, miss!" Dr. Forsythe, a tall man of perhaps fifty, with very pale blue eyes behind his thick bifocal spectacles, leaned forward to see her better. He had a trim beard and sported a thick set of muttonchop sideburns, but his domed head had nary a hair and seemed like a perfect vessel for all the fascinating knowledge he had collected over his years of Arctic travel.

"Curiously enough, because of the strong westerly winds and currents, some of those Inuit in their sealskin boats were pulled out to sea and fetched up on the western coasts of Ireland and on Scotland's outermost islands." Dr. Forsythe's pale eyes sparkled with a new light behind the thick lenses. "And what would the Scottish lass walking on the beach with her beau find?" A hush had fallen on the small group. "What would they think at the sight of a man sitting upright and rigid in his *umiak*? The boat in perfect condition and the man seemingly perfect as well. For he was flawlessly preserved, that is, in death."

There was a gasp from the small audience. "Yes, amazing, isn't it? A man in a sealskin boat, enshrouded in his sealskin parka. A 'seal man,' as they began to call these people who died in the icy embrace of the winter sea when blown from their course. His ship had become his coffin. And thus indeed, there was a confluence of two worlds — that of the spirit and that of the temporal, or corporeal." Dr. Forsythe was looking right at Lucy now. It was almost as if no one else was in the gallery.

"What do you mean?" she whispered.

"*Selkies*? Do you know the word?"

Lucy shook her head. She waited almost breathlessly for his answer.

"The mythological shape-shifting creatures, seal folk, who are said to be seals in the sea but humans upon the land. The origins of these legends were based upon these Inuit fishermen who got caught out at sea in their sealskin boats."

"Legend?" Lucy asked.

"Yes, legend." Dr. Forsythe rocked back on his heels. "Or maybe it's just a spirit revealed." The doctor blinked, and a quiet seemed suddenly to engulf them. Everyone else had moved on to another display.

"THE THICK"

"OH, LUCY! LUCY! The grandest news! You'll never believe it!" Marjorie squealed as Lucy stepped into the foyer.

Lucy was shocked that the first words out of her mother's mouth were not about the reception. She usually bombarded Lucy with questions upon her return from any gathering. Whom did she see? Whom did she talk to? What did she talk about? The irony was that although Lucy often struggled to think of conversation topics on the spot, after the fact she was very good at thinking up all sorts of things she could have or should have said.

"What is it, Mother?"

"Mrs. Simpson is coming soon," she said, glancing at the hallway mirror and smoothing her hair.

"That's your news?" Lucy tried not to sound too deflated, although she didn't understand why the arrival of the seamstress would be newsworthy.

Mrs. Simpson usually made two visits a year to prepare their dresses. Much to Marjorie Snow's regret, they could not afford the thrice-yearly visits that were the norm for wealthier families. It seemed unfair since being the wife of a cleric in the high Episcopal Church demanded that the family constantly be on display, not only at church on Sundays but also at the numerous other ecclesiastical occasions including funerals, weddings, and the ladies' altar guild meetings.

"Yes, I know we've already had her, but we need new clothes, and we'll just have to somehow cover the costs." She paused and inhaled deeply as if she required more air to accommodate this next announcement. "Lucy darling, your father has been asked to become the summer minister in Bar Harbor, Maine, at the Episcopal church. The Little Chapel by the Sea, they call it. Doesn't that sound quaint?"

"By the sea," Lucy murmured. She closed her eyes for just a moment and once more tried to recall the Arctic sea and that enigmatic, luminous greenish light. Was the water green or was it the light or both? she thought.

"Yes, darling, Bar Harbor is on the island of Mount Desert. Next to Newport, there is not a better summer resort. It's where all the best people go. Newport really borders on the garish. You know, new-money types." Marjorie's nostrils pinched together as if she had picked up the whiff of something slightly rancid. "But Bar Harbor — you can't beat it. Rockefellers and Astors from New York, Hawleys and Peabodys and Cabots from Boston. Oh, the very finest. Do you realize what this means, Lucy?"

"It means we'll live close to the ocean!"

"Well, yes, dear, that, too. But it also means that you'll have many opportunities to meet lovely young people and go to dances and teas and yachting. And your father will be rubbing shoulders with many of the gentlemen who influence the nominations for the bishop of New York. We all know that Bishop Vanderwaker is literally on his last leg since the amputation. Diabetes, poor thing." She paused and clicked her tongue, producing a fretting sound suggesting deep concern, or at least the semblance of deep concern. "He usually takes the pulpit in Bar Harbor, but not this year."

Her mother gave a tight little smile and then seemed to think better and arranged her face to suggest a more sympathetic sensibility.

Lucy, too, could hardly suppress her own elation. To live by the sea, not in a city hemmed in by two rather dirty old rivers that seemed far from the open ocean, was a dream come true.

"Oh, this is wonderful, Mother, just wonderful!"

Marjorie seldom saw her normally sedate daughter given to such exuberant displays. She embraced her warmly and pressed her cheek to Lucy's face. She almost had to stand on tiptoes now to do so, since her daughter had shot up several inches over the past year.

"I'm so happy you're happy, Lucy dear." She then took a step away, still holding her daughter's hands, and spoke. "There are so many nice young people there. So high class. And you're growing into such a beauty! Just look at you. Why, only the other day at church Mrs. Morton commented on it."

"Oh, Mother, really," Lucy said, pulling away. If her mother or anyone else had heard that stupid exchange with Eldon Drexel, or her remark about Charles Worth, they would not think of her as anything but a very awkward girl.

"Don't 'oh, Mother' me, dear. You're a prize."

A prize, Lucy thought. It sounded like a cheap toy given for knocking down all the pins at a carnival game. But she said nothing and merely smiled.

"So," her mother continued, "Mrs. Simpson is coming to make up some summer frocks for us."

"But, Mother, she already came to make our summer frocks. I have enough."

"No, dear, not just afternoon dresses and things like that. You know how dead New York is in the summer. There is no season to speak of. No parties, dances, not anything. It's absolutely stultifying. But in Bar Harbor, it's a different story entirely. All the fine families have ballrooms in their cottages. We need summer gowns."

As her mother prattled on, Lucy wondered how many occasions she'd have to appear like an absolute fool on this island. After all, a ball by the sea was still a ball. Though the notion of cottages with ball-rooms seemed odd. "Mother, how can a cottage have space enough for a ballroom?"

"They call them 'cottages,' but they are very large."

"Then why don't they call them mansions?" She suppressed a sigh. Sometimes, it felt like New York society spoke an entirely different language.

"Well, you know, it's a summer place, a resort. They don't want to show off, not like those people in Newport. They are a little more subdued in Bar Harbor, less formal."

Lucy said nothing. She was thrilled that she would be going so close to the sea, but all this talk of balls and parties had triggered a welter of anxiety that burbled up inside her. She felt almost queasy.

At that moment a bell rang. "Mercy, it's Mrs. Simpson." There was the patter of feet as Mary Ann, their maid, hurried to the door. "Now go upstairs, darling, and get down to your petticoats. Then come to my bedroom, and Mrs. Simpson will be in to mea-sure you. We'll look at the fabrics she's brought."

"Yes, Mother." But she headed to her father's study first.

"Where are you going, dear?"

"Just to Father's study. I want to fetch something. He's not meeting with anyone, is he?"

"No, he's still at church, meeting with some committee. But, Lucy, don't get lost in some book. I know how that happens to you."

But of course she did get lost in a book. Lucy took an atlas to her bedroom upstairs and had only half undressed when she found the map she wanted. Taking a ruler first, she calculated the distance in inches — which she realized was rather stupid — between Greenland and the islands called the Hebrides that Dr. Forsythe had spoken of. From Cape Farewell to the Outer Hebrides was about four inches on the map. From Maine, it was at least six.

"Lucy! Lucy!" Her mother's fluting voice carried down the hallway. "Lucy, Mrs. Simpson is here."

"Just a minute. I'll be there." The map in the atlas

did not show Bar Harbor. All she knew was that the island was on the coast north of Portland, not too far from the Canadian border. She would have to go to the public library for better maps. She heard the footsteps coming down the hall.

"Really, Lucy! Mrs. Simpson is here. It's rude to keep her waiting. She's made a special trip and brought so many fabrics."

"All right! All right! I'm coming."

Lucy shut the atlas and followed her mother down the hall into the master bedroom. The bed was all but obliterated as a tidal wave of fabric surged across it.

"It's such a shame that we don't have a larger space for you to spread these out, Mrs. Simpson, but you know we're church people. We're not like one of your uptown clients, say, Mrs. Bannister. I'm sure she has an expansive boudoir in her Fifth Avenue mansion."

"Now, don't you fret, Mrs. Snow." Mrs. Simpson, a stout woman, was holding a swath of fabric up to the tip of her nose and extending her arm. "I must have at least five yards of this lawn cotton. That'll do you for the tea dances. Lawn fabric — nothing like it. Liberty's the department store in London. They sell it. I have my sources over here, you know." She winked. Mrs. Simpson was a great one for winking. "And it's the perfect thing to wear in Bar Harbor. You don't want to be too fancy, you know, for a tea dance."

"They have tea dances, then, on the island?" Marjorie Snow asked.

"Oh, you betcha. They got themselves a pavilion for it. The dances go from four to six in the afternoon. That gives you a couple of hours after the tennis games." She nodded knowingly at Lucy.

Lucy doubted that she would be much good at tennis, but her mother seemed so happy, and she did not want to spoil her anticipation.

"You know so much, Mrs. Simpson, about Bar Harbor and the life there," Marjorie Snow said with a sigh.

"Well, I got more than a dozen clients that go every summer." She had finished measuring the lawn cotton fabric and was folding it. "Let's see — the Van Wycks, the Benedicts, the Bellamys, the Astors."

"The Astors!"

"Oh, yes. Been sewing for Mrs. A for almost five years now."

"My goodness!" Marjorie exclaimed as if she had just glimpsed one of the seven wonders of the world. "Oh, and, Mrs. Simpson, I nearly forgot. I think Lucy needs some combinations."

"But, Mother, I have so many chemises and drawers."

"Now, Lucy." Mrs. Simpson shook her finger. "You want to have the slimmest silhouette possible. Separate chemises and drawers are a thing of the past. You must let me whip up some combis for you. I have the prettiest pink pearl — mind you, not real pearl — for the chemise top buttons. You'll love them. And I can run a little ribbon through for decoration. You'll look slim as a reed. No bunching up of the drawers and chemise. So figure hugging. And that's what we're after, isn't it?"

"Of course," Lucy murmured.

Mrs. Simpson continued. "Now, for the evening affairs, it's a bit fancier. A bit of a show, but nothing gaudy like them Newport families. All these folks come up from Boston and they got a bit of the Puritan in them. Matter of fact, I just made Mrs. Astor a dress inspired — mind you inspired, not copied — from a Charles Frederick Worth design. Gorgeous green chiffon with a cascading back. Looks like waves from the sea."

"Oh, I'd like that!" Lucy said.

"Well, dearie, 'fraid I can't make you one. Wouldn't do for you to show up in something like Mrs. Astor's gown. But I've got plenty of ideas. Plenty of fabrics. So let's get to work. When did you say you leave?"

"Three weeks. First of June," Marjorie answered. "They want us there early, unfashionably early, I suppose. Most likely the important people don't get there until later."

"Yes, that's so. First big round of parties begins late June."

"Oh, I do hope we'll get invited." Marjorie pressed her lips together and raised her eyebrows as if she dared not say more.

"Of course you'll get invited. You're the parson's wife." Mrs. Simpson turned to Lucy. "And the parson's daughter."

Lucy saw her mother wince. Marjorie Snow loathed the term *parson*. It made them all sound like country bumpkins. Or, worse yet, confirmed her secret terror of living on the edges of society instead of in its midst. She did not want to be included merely because she was a minister's wife, but for her own merits. She was from Baltimore after all, and although Prissy was perhaps not a true blood relative, they were as close as any sisters, despite the differences in their backgrounds. Their lives in fact had fallen into an odd synchronism, for they had been born within a month of each other, and each had lost a parent shortly after her birth. After Marjorie's father died, Marjorie and her mother, Rose, were invited to move into a cottage on the Bancroft estate, seeing as Rose had been Prissy's mother Adelia's best friend. The two girls seemed destined also to become best friends and were inseparable until their respective marriages at twenty-one.

Neither Marjorie nor Prissy had been blessed with conceiving a child. Marjorie and Stephen had decided to adopt, but Priscilla could not, owing to certain legal entailments from the Bancroft estate.

Marjorie and Priscilla remained fast friends throughout the years, and Priscilla often bestowed upon them modest sums of money and never missed sending presents for Lucy.

Yet Marjorie was pleased when they moved to New York for Stephen to take the pulpit of St. Luke's. Despite her friendship with Priscilla, they really weren't anybody in Baltimore, for Southerners had long memories, and as the old families went, she and her widowed mother, Rose, had been little more than "dependents." Slightly above servants but still charity cases with no real background.

So when Marjorie and Stephen moved to New York five years after their marriage, it was as if the slate were wiped clean. She could talk about her dear friend Priscilla Bancroft Devries, but people didn't know the details and she need not inform them — although she was inclined sometimes to elaborate a bit. New Yorkers weren't quite so passionate about genealogy as Southerners were.

When Stephen had told her of the opportunity to adopt Lucy, Marjorie had one stipulation — no one must know that she was adopted. Not even Priscilla.

She did not want any "entailments" interfering with her daughter's chance for a brilliant marriage. And now there was this chance, the wonderful opportunity to be on an island with some of America's richest families. It wouldn't be like New York. The parish of St. Luke's was respectable enough, but its standing was somewhat diluted because of its location so far downtown. Nevertheless, it was a springboard to the office of the bishop, just as Bar Harbor would serve as a springboard for Lucy's marital prospects. And then there would be no more teetering on the terrifying edges. They would be in the thick of it, or "the thick," as Marjorie Snow sometimes thought of it.

THE EDGE

UNTIL BRIDGEPORT, the glimpses of water had been brief, but now the views became more expansive, especially as they entered Rhode Island. Lucy kept her face pressed to the window. A sensation had begun to build in her. This was no mere train ride. When she looked out the window, it was not simply a coastline that unspooled before her but an edge, and she was being drawn close to that edge. It dared her in a sense — or was it beckoning her?

Lucy sat across from her mother and father in a private compartment on the New York–New Haven–Hartford railroad. The click of her mother's knitting needles occasionally surfaced amidst the cacophony of the train's wheezes, groans, and clanking wheels.

Her father was browsing through old sermons, or so she supposed, until she heard him say, "Marjorie, the Althorps apparently have a cottage on Bar Harbor."

"Really, dear? The downtown Althorps or the uptown ones?"

"The downtown ones. Edward and Felicity of our congregation."

"Well, I never thought they had the means."

"Nor did I, but here they are listed as members of the tennis club."

"Oh, Lucy, I do hope you'll take some tennis lessons." Marjorie dropped her knitting in her lap. "Lucy, did you hear me?"

"Huh?" Her eyes were fastened on the expanse of gray-green water of a deep bay.

"Oh, Lucy, don't say 'huh.' That is so coarse."

"Sorry, Mother. What were you saying?"

"I said I hope you will take tennis lessons."

"Oh, Mother, I don't think I'd be very good. You know, my foot and all." Lucy tried to imagine herself chasing a ball on a tennis court, stumbling about in much the same manner she did in conversations at parties with people like the Ogmonts and the Drexels. She could imagine Denise De Becque, Elsie Ogmont, and Lenora Drexel in their tennis whites snickering at her, and felt a twinge in her stomach.

"Nonsense!" her father boomed. Stephen Snow was speaking in a voice he seldom used in the pulpit but often used in his home when contradicting either his wife or Lucy. "Your foot is so much better. Vastly improved, and the only way to keep improving is to try new things. There are such opportunities in store for you, Lucy. You must not squander them."

"Absolutely! Listen to your father, dear!" Marjorie Snow had resumed her knitting. "Like dancing. You've danced before. Such opportunities . . ."

Tennis, dancing — opportunities for marriage, Lucy thought as she returned her gaze to the coastline. The train seemed to be devouring the track, and the coastline fled by, but then new vistas would open up, and the boundless sea stretched before her.

"I'm so glad, Stephen," Marjorie Snow said as she picked up a dropped stitch, "that the church decided to pay for first-class compartments on the train and the steamer."

"First class all the way. We have to arrive in style, for the good of St. Luke's. We must reflect well on our church. They don't invite just any Episcopal priest to go to the Little Chapel by the Sea."

"Yes, of course. And you see, Lucy, that is why you must enter into all the young people's activities. We must all reflect well."

"We are emissaries of the church," her father said, rather grandly.

"You mean like missionaries?" Lucy asked.

"Heavens, no!" her mother exclaimed. "We aren't here to proselytize. Good gracious. It's Bar Harbor, not Africa! Father was saying that we must reflect well on the church. We must shine. Be our best."

Lucy was trying to process what her parents were saying. It sounded like a fashion show. She pictured an immense oval mirror holding the reflections of the three of them in their new summer wardrobes. Her father in his summer clerics. Herself in one of the lawn cotton tea dance dresses, and her mother in her walking suit. The images changed — new outfits. Her father in his formal dress clerics for an evening event, her mother in an evening gown of ice blue silk, and herself in a ball gown of sea-foam green silk and lace that Mrs. Simpson said set off the deep green of her eyes.

There was a sudden knocking on their compartment door.

The Reverend Snow stood up and opened the door. It was the conductor. "Next stop Boston, South Station. Porter will meet you on the platform with your trunks. You've booked a cab?"

"Yes, sir. My secretary made the arrangements for our transport to the steamer dock in the harbor."

"Fine, fine, Reverend." The conductor seemed to linger a moment. Lucy saw her father jerk to attention.

"Oh!" His hand reached in his pocket. She saw him pull out a half-dollar coin. He flushed slightly as the conductor took the coin.

As soon as the door closed, Marjorie Snow whispered, "A half-dollar, Stephen?"

"We can't appear cheap, my dear," he said brightly. "We are going to be consorting with Van Wycks, Astors, Bellamys — the whole lot!"

Lucy's parents beamed at each other. They had never appeared more ecstatic.

And she, too, felt a thrill surge through her as she stepped off the train. She sniffed the air. The scent of the sea threaded through the coal fumes of the loco-motive's steamy belches. Salt air! One never caught such a scent in New York.

She inhaled deeply as they followed the porter with their four steamer trunks. She ran a bit ahead to catch up with the fellow.

"Pardon me, sir, but how close are we to the sea?"

"The habber?" he asked. She realized that he meant *harbor*, but with his thick Boston accent, the *r* had vanished.

"Yes, sir."

"Not far, missy. Take the cab twenty minutes but that's because of the traffic. Less than half a mile to Lincoln wharf, where you catch the steamuh." He had a plain-as-pudding face, and his hair, which stuck out under his cap, was the color of pale carrots. She detected a slight Irish lilt, which she found lovely.

When they arrived at the wharf, she was nearly overwhelmed with the most marvelous sensations. She took off her bonnet, faced into the breeze, and flung back her head. A hairpin came undone and the carefully wound bun fell loose, cascading in ripples down her back. The wind caught it and whipped it in streams across her face.

"Lucy, for heaven's sake, what are you doing, child? Your hat! Your bun!"

"Oh, Mother, doesn't this air feel wonderful? And look, you can really see the ocean from Boston." They were standing near the end of the wharf where the *Elizabeth M. Prouty*, the coastal steamer, lay against the pilings, bobbing gently. This was the ship that would take them across Massachusetts Bay, up the coast of New Hampshire, across Casco Bay, Muscongus, then Penobscot Bay, and finally into Frenchman's Bay and Mount Desert Island.

"What's this?" Her father took one look at her and gasped. He appeared mortified, as if she had stripped off all her clothes and was standing naked on the wharf. Surely the absence of her hat and the sight of her disheveled hair could not be that unnerving.

"What is wrong?" Lucy asked, worried by her parents' transfixed expressions.

"You look so different," her mother said, staring at her as if she were a stranger. Lucy's hair, touched by the sun, was a flaming conflagration, and her eyes sparkled a fierce green.

"Ain't she a looker!" A stevedore whistled low and then suddenly the air was crosshatched with such whistles.

"Come along, child, it's time to board. And for God's sake, put your hat on." It was more a prayer than a curse that her father uttered as he grabbed her arm and steered her toward the gangplank.

The wind was on their nose, which was unusual for this time of year, and the captain informed them that, due to the contrary breezes, they would arrive at six the next morning. Lucy couldn't have been happier. The longer she could be at sea, the better. She did not plan on sleeping a wink. Why spend any time in a stuffy cabin when one could be outdoors? Her parents might worry if they knew her plans, so it would be best if she did not tell them. She had firmly decided that she would try her best to be the model daughter, the perfect emissary. She would even agree to give tennis a try if it would really help her father's designs to become bishop of the diocese of New York.

And she was the perfect daughter that night, going down to dinner in the ship's dining salon in a gray cashmere dress with a fitted jacket. They were seated at the captain's table and the captain, Andrew Burch, asked that the reverend give the blessing. Marjorie was pleased with the honor but slightly disappointed that there was no one of note at the table. It was too early, as Mrs. Simpson had said, for the summer people. There was a dentist and his wife who were disembarking in Portland, a businessman and his ten-year-old son, also from Portland, and a governess who had come in advance of another family — the Greens — whom Marjorie had never heard of but who apparently summered in Bar Harbor.

The talk was mostly about weather, and though Marjorie attempted to ask the governess a few discreet questions about the Greens, she was able to extract precious little information. At the conclusion of the dinner, they bid their tablemates farewell and wished them all a good summer.

The Snows' cabin was a double suite, thanks once again to the largess of St. Luke's, and when they had returned, Marjorie sank down on a settee and sighed. "Now I hope I don't get seasick." The ship was rolling a bit as they had steamed beyond the deep bays of the Massachusetts coastline and were exposed to the open sea. "My goodness, Lucy, how do you stand there and keep your balance without holding on to anything?"

Lucy shrugged. She loved the rhythm of the waves; it was as if she had known this motion all her life. She felt almost cradled by it. But how could she explain any of her feelings to her parents, who both looked a bit queasy? She tried to change the subject.

"Mother, you said good-bye to Miss Burnham, the governess, as if we'll never see her again this summer. Surely our paths will cross."

She saw her mother and father exchange glances. "Oh, I don't think her employers are our kind, dear," her father answered quickly.

"Mr. and Mrs. Green?"

"Yes." Her mother coughed slightly. "It's an . . . iffy name?"

"What? Whatever do you mean?"

"Well, you know . . ." She lifted her short, thin eyebrows, which arched steeply like tiny commas over her somewhat vague hazel eyes. Her lips clamped together as if she preferred silence to any sort of explanation.

"Your mother is trying to say . . . that these are not our kind of people. The . . . the name suggests a different race."

"A different race?" Lucy asked.

"Jews — possibly." This comment took Lucy aback. She had never heard her parents speak this way. It was something she could imagine someone like Denise De Becque saying, or Eldon Drexel. But her parents, particularly her father, were quite careful in how they spoke of other faiths.

A different race? What exactly did that mean? Lucy wondered. It was a religion, she thought — but a race? She was confused. She had seen Jews in New York, met some. The cobbler, Mr. Hurwitz, was Jewish. So was the lady in the New York Public Library at the reference desk. Miss Gold was her name. She had been very helpful. They perhaps looked slightly different, but so did the Irish porter who had carried their trunks in the station, and so did Anna, the Swedish lady who cooked for them. But would you say they were different races? She thought about how her parents had stared at her on the wharf when she had removed her hat — their shocked countenances. It was as if she had not been stripped naked but become something else entirely — another race, another being, something not quite human — an alien apparition.

These disturbing thoughts lingered with Lucy as she crawled into her bunk. Although she had no intention of sleeping, the rocking motion of the steamer, the swells rolling in from the vast Atlantic, were seductive. Despite the dull thrumming of the engines, she could still hear the hypnotic rhythm of the crush of the sea against the hull.

I don't want to play tennis. I want to swim. No one had ever taught her, but she did not doubt that she could swim. She simply knew it.

As she drifted off to sleep, she thought about the Begats, the little doll family that inhabited the doll-house Aunt Prissy had given her. Lucy had invented the Begats long before she ever discovered those papers in her father's study, her adoption papers from St. Luke's with the words "mother unknown." So had she wondered even then who had begat her? Who was "mother unknown"?

She had always listened so carefully in church when her father read the verses from Matthew. She had loved the rhythm, the cadences, as the people, starting with Abraham, then Isaac, Jacob, and Judas, tumbled out of that cataract that was Jesus' original family. And the names became odder as the people, all of whom seemed to be men, were born. There was Aminadab after Aram and then Nassoon and Salmon and Booz. Occasionally a girl or woman was mentioned. In Lucy's Begat family, it was just the opposite — mostly girls and sometimes a boy.

Lucy's eyes began to close. Her kin were not mythical. Somewhere, they really did exist and they had begat Lucy. Was this the edge she was approaching, a precipice over which she might peek and discover who she was and from where she had come? Discover her kind?

Lucy sat bolt upright in her bunk. How could she have fallen asleep? Peering through the porthole, she could see two stars. Thank heaven it was still night. There was still time to go up on deck. She could hear the soft snores of her parents in the adjoining cabin suite. The ship was moving smoothly now. There was very little rocking motion. The wind must have died down. She put on her warmest coat, added a thick shawl, and slipped out of the cabin.

As she stepped on deck, she knew she had stepped up to the brink, the elusive edge of another world. Wrapped in the light breeze, the scent of the sea, she gasped as she saw the wobbling reflection of the moon on the water. Tears started to stream down her face. She wondered why she was crying. She had never been happier and yet the world suddenly felt fragile to her, as fragile as that quivering reflection.

VIEW FROM THE LIGHTHOUSE.

GAR PLUM LEANED against the rail of the circular walkway on the outside of the lighthouse that he tended. The signature of the light was two one-second flashes every ten seconds. It was in this ten-second interval of darkness that he could catch a glimpse of her, his daughter May, her tail lifting like a waterborne comet from sea to sky. What he had known yet denied for years, from the time he had first fetched her from that sea chest floating offshore, had been confirmed nine months earlier, in September, when he first caught sight of her swimming straight out to sea on a blustery night. It had taken him that long to accept the inevitable — that his May, his dear May, belonged to the sea. They were as close as any father and natural-born daughter could be. And yet he could not bring himself to confess that he knew her secret. He had rehearsed it in his mind so many times, but it always came out wrong, as if he were forgiving her for being what she was. There was no need for forgiveness. He often wondered what would have happened if he had not found her. Would she have died? Had he really rescued her? Or had he committed her to a life of suffering shut up in this lighthouse?

"Crossing over" — that was how he had thought of May's transformation. She hadn't always been this way, or rather, she had not always known that other secret part of her self. He was pretty sure it had happened a year or more ago. The previous spring when the last nor'easter blew through. She'd kept it a secret, though, even from Hugh, her beau from Cambridge — a Harvard man. He wondered if Hugh would be back this summer.

There! He saw it. The dazzling tail lifting from a swirl of phosphorescence. She was a quarter mile out. The light's sweeping flash blurred the colors that were more beautiful than any rainbow. *Where did she go?* he wondered. What would he do if he lost her? Would she someday swim away forever?

May could hear the thumping reverberations of the *Elizabeth M. Prouty* coming through the passage between Egg Rock and Bar Harbor. *No more acrobatics,* she thought to herself. She didn't want to attract the attention of any crewmembers on deck or the pilot who stood on the prow. She was about to dive straight to the bottom, but then the void that so often pressed against her left side began to quiver, then pulsate with a stronger beat. Once there had been two such voids pressing against her, but the one on her right side had disappeared after she found her sister, Hannah Albury, at the end of the previous summer. She and Hannah had discovered each other while swimming right in the center, the windless eye, of the hurricane. May had felt that pulsing in the void just moments before they had caught sight of each other. Soon after meeting, May and Hannah became convinced that there was a third sister. Could she be coming now? May could hardly contain her excitement as her flukes twitched with anticipation.

May felt the flutter in her stomach harden into concern. What if she was rich and snooty? What would she think of a sister who lived in a lighthouse? Who owned only three dresses that had been patched and repatched so often that her summer one made her look like a walking quilt? At least Hannah, who served in a rich family's house, had some sense of the finer things — like finger bowls and harp music. But May knew none of this. She had grown up in almost perfect isolation on this small island, only venturing into town to attend school or visit the library.

May knew it was wrong of her to assume that all rich people were snooty. Hannah said that little Ettie Hawley was the sweetest person ever. But it was one thing to be friendly with your employer's young daughter. It was quite another to build a relationship with the sister you've never met — who might not even know that she *had* sisters.

She was very close. May sensed it. Perhaps she was on the deck of the *Prouty*. May dove and swam deep beneath the keel stream of the steamer. She could not tear herself away. She knew the girl was on that ship and she had to follow it.

She'd experienced a similar sensation when she and Hannah had made the long swim to the shipwreck of the *Resolute* and found where their parents had died. It was as if they had been pulled toward the long-lost shadows of kin. One did not need a compass; one was just inexorably drawn. May had begun to call these instincts the Laws of Salt. They were not mere passing urges but something more primal, and they told May that one who had crossed over could not approach one who had not.

May and Hannah were mer. The salt flowed through their veins, but if this sister had not yet completed the transformation, she had to be allowed to find her own way to the sea.

☙ ☙ ☙

May left the keel stream and began to swim quietly next to the *Prouty*, just inches beneath the surface of the water, disturbing it no more than a small school of fish. She moved alongside for several minutes, then swam aft and followed in the white curl of the wake, rolling over onto her back so she could try to spot her on deck.

When nothing was revealed aft, she swam toward the prow. It took no effort at all for her to keep up with the steamer. Just as May rolled onto her back again, she glimpsed her. It was her hair really that caught her eye. It swirled around her head like a pale fire in the night.

The Laws of Salt did not, however, prevent May from telling Hannah. She couldn't wait. She hoped Hannah came swimming tonight instead of spending the evening with that painter. He was so — She broke off the thought. She had no right to think such things. And it was not that she thought ill of the painter Stannish Wheeler. Not really. There was just something about him that she found slightly — what was the word she was looking for? — *disquieting.*

A COTTAGE BY THE SEA

"**Watch the tree roots.** They bump up and we wouldn't want you to trip, Reverend and Mrs. Snow. Elmer, you and Petey go easy with that trunk. It ain't a cah of bugs."

"Ayuh, don't worry none, Elva."

"Bugs?" Lucy asked as they followed Elva Perry through the woodland path.

"Ha! Forgot myself, de-ah. Bugs is just a local name for lobstah."

Does no one ever pronounce the letter r *in New England?* Lucy thought. But she had never been happier. The woodland path had begun to thread its way through the pines and spruce closer to the sea. She could hear the crush of the waves. Scraps of fog hung in the branches like vaporous scarves of chiffon.

"She be comin' in thick as mud, ain't she?" Elmer called back. "Won't be able to see the cove by the time we get to the cottage."

But I can smell it, Lucy thought. *I can feel it.* There was a tang in the air as the salt mingled with the piney scent of the woods.

Lucy glanced at Marjorie. She could see her bottom lip quivering. "It's all right, Mother. It's all so lovely after the city and the smell of fumes and all."

"But so rustic and rather remote."

"Remote?"

"How long have we been walking?"

"Not five minutes, Mother. Even less from the churchyard to here. It's so beautiful. I can't wait to do some watercolor and ink drawings of all this."

"You paint, de-ah?" Elva Perry asked.

"A bit." In truth Lucy had thought a lot about painting the sea ever since she had seen the exhibit at the natural history museum. She marveled at the colors the museum scene painters had come up with, and was anxious to see how the sea might be colored by the sky, the light of sun on water. If the day was cloudy, would the sea turn gray?

"Oh, she's quite accomplished, our Lucy," the Reverend Snow said, smiling.

"You know, we got one of the country's greatest painters who comes here most every summer," Elva said.

"Who might that be?" Marjorie Snow asked.

"Stannish Whitman Wheeler."

"Stannish Whitman Wheeler!" the two elder Snows exclaimed.

"I can't believe it!" Marjorie gasped.

"Oh, yes. He comes to paint all the rich people's portraits — Astors, Rockefellers, Bellamys, Benedicts, Hawleys. You name it."

"He painted Bishop Vanderwaker," Marjorie said.

"Indeed he did!" Elva said. "Loveliest man who ever walked the earth." She then inhaled sharply. "Oh, de-ah! What a thing for me to say. Guess he isn't doing much walking now that he lost that leg."

"Yes, so sad," Marjorie chirped. Although these were kind words, the alacrity of her response undercut any true compassion. "Now, tell me, Mrs. Perry, how far to the Quoddy Tennis and Bathing Club that we passed?"

"Maybe ten minutes."

"Don't worry, Mother," Lucy said as Marjorie grimaced. "Nothing can be so far. We're on an island. And they said there is a buckboard and one of the church deacon's servants will drive us anywhere we want to go."

"Yes, that's nice." Marjorie was silent for a few seconds. "I — I —" she stammered.

"What, Mother?"

Marjorie dropped her voice a bit. "I just wonder if we mightn't have done better to take rooms at that hotel, the St. Sauveur, we passed on the main avenue? They say a very smart set goes there."

"My dear," the reverend interrupted. "Firstly, they do not call the streets here avenues, they are just streets or roads. And secondly, it is customary for the minister of a church to live in the rectory, not a hotel." Just as he spoke the word *hotel*, a stone cottage appeared behind a scrim of blue spruce trees. Its foundation was buried in thickets of ferns, and ivy scrambled up its granite walls. The shutters were painted a dark bluish green to match the spruce.

"Now come round for the real view," Elva Perry said. "Won't have you going in through the kitchen door."

As they rounded the house, the damp east wind smacked them in the face. "Look to the north quick before it gets swallowed by the fog. That be Mount Abenaki — said to be the first place that the sun strikes on the continent!"

Lucy stood on the porch of the little stone house. She heard her father say, "How fascinating." It was the same empty tone he used when he baptized a rather unattractive baby and said "how handsome" for boys or "how engaging" for girls.

"I guess you'd say I'm a bit *pahshul* myself. Me being part Indian, you know."

"Excuse me?" Marjorie nearly yelped.

"Ayuh — most of us round here have a bit of Indian blood — Scots and Irish, 'course them folk come down from Nova Scotia, but Indian Penobscot, Passamaquoddy, or Abenaki, most of us have a bit of that." Elva wove her long hands through the tendrils of fog swirling about them. "We mix it all up here."

Lucy saw her mother blanch, becoming as white as the fog. Elva continued, "Over at the Mount Desert Canoe Club, they always got a few Indians to show summer folk how to paddle a canoe."

The luminous seascape with the Inuit skimming across the water flashed through Lucy's mind's eye. "Oh, Mother, I'd much rather take canoe lessons than tennis lessons."

"Absolutely not!" Then under her breath, Lucy heard her mother mutter something about how Indians certainly would not be teaching tennis.

Elva Perry took out a key, unlatched the door, and held it wide open so Elmer and Petey could carry in the trunk.

"We'll get the rest of the baggage in a jiff," Elmer said as the Reverend Snow and his wife followed them in. However, Lucy lingered on the porch and looked out toward the sea.

"You still out here, hey? Can't see much now with the fog rolling in," Elmer said.

"Where are we on the island exactly?"

"This here is round the bend from where the *Prouty* came in. You're on a southwest corner. Just above Otter Creek."

"Do people go swimming out there?" She nodded toward the ocean. Although it was cloaked in thick fog, she could hear the waves.

Petey laughed. "You mean out there in the ocean?"

"Yes, where else?"

"Water's awfully cold, and there are some wicked big currents. Not really safe. Kids swim off the town wharf all the time, and it's nice going swimming in the ponds, but no. No one goes swimming out there."

But Lucy was sure they were wrong. When she had come on deck on the *Prouty*, she had felt a presence in the water just before dawn, so close by it was as if she could have leaned over the rail and touched it. Someone had been swimming just beneath the surface, and at one point, she thought she caught a shimmering form, but then it had vanished, leaving Lucy with an emptiness that ached deep within her.

"Lucy! Where are you?" her father called out.

"I'm coming!" She walked through the door. It was a charming parlor. Elva Perry was explaining the intricacies of the wood-burning stove that heated the downstairs. "And I got some chowdah heating up on the cookstove. You only need this heat stove when it's foggy like this morning. Takes the damp out of things, but you can shut it down if the sun comes out. Easy as pie really, but I'll be coming down every day and can help you out." Then she tapped her head as if to remind herself of something. "Oh, yes. There's the rat poisoning up there on the top shelf in the kitchen."

"Rats! There are rats?" Marjorie Snow's eyes seemed to bulge out from their sockets.

"No, de-ah. Not bad as that. But red squirrels sometimes get into the walls from the outside. If you hear any scurrying around, just tell me. No need to fool with it yourself. I felt it was safest to put it on that high shelf. I wasn't sure if you had youngsters who might get into it. Best it be out of reach."

"That was very thoughtful of you, Mrs. Perry," the Reverend Snow said.

"Yes, well, one can't be too careful. If you need anything, just holler. No telephones down here. Very few on the island to tell you the truth. Just in the grand cottages."

"Hardly a grand cottage here," Marjorie said through clenched teeth. "No electricity. No phone. And the threat of invading squirrels. All quite rustic."

"Oh, that's the way Bishop Vanderwaker wanted it. He loved this place, so when the Peabodys offered to install modern conveniences, he said no, absolutely not! He always quoted Matthew, chapter nineteen."

"Ah!" the Reverend Snow exclaimed softly. "It is easier for a camel to go through the eye of a needle than for a rich man to enter into the kingdom of God."

"Yes, sir. He is a plain man. We miss him."

"I can assure you we need no embellishments. This cottage is perfect the way it is. We are honored to be here and will try and follow in the distinguished steps of our esteemed predecessor, Bishop Vanderwaker."

Lucy could tell her father was set on delivering a sermon, so she was thankful for the arrival of Elmer and Petey with the last of the trunks.

"Now there's a real steep path," Elmer said as he put down the trunk. "It winds down from the cottage here to the sea. But it's slippery and dangerous and not much of a beach. If it's a beach you want, go down to the Quoddy Tennis and Bathing Club. That's the best place."

"Oh, yes. That's what we'll do," Marjorie said enthusiastically. "I bought Lucy a very fine bathing costume."

It was the ugliest thing she had ever seen. Lucy shuddered as she thought about the horrible mustard-colored yellow canvas skirt, which hung just below her knees and under which she was to wear thick black stockings.

"You know," Elva said. "A lot of the women are wearing the new style with bloomers under the skirts, or just plain trousers with a blouse."

Marjorie squared her shoulders. "Mrs. Simpson, our seamstress, assured me that the canvas or wool dress style was most appropriate."

"Yes, they still wear them, too. But hardly anyone gets into the seawater. Wicked cold, you know. They go in the club pool. Oh my goodness, time's gotten away from me. I'm due at the Hawleys."

"The Hawleys!" Marjorie exclaimed. "The Boston Hawleys?"

"Only ones I know. They be coming in next week, and I always go and help with the airing out of Gladrock."

"Gladrock?"

"Their cottage. Probably the prettiest on all of Mount Desert. Which reminds me." Elva Perry wheeled about and looked straight at Lucy. "They got a maid over there and if she ain't the spittin' image of you, de-ah! Same red hair, perhaps a shade or two darker. You could be sisters."

Marjorie gave a shrill little laugh. A muscle near her left eye flinched. It was an odd little tic that afflicted her occasionally.

"Really?" Lucy said. "Well, I hope I have occasion to meet her sometime."

"She's a serving girl, dear," Marjorie said. Her pulpy face settled into an expression of mild consternation. Lucy had seen that expression before, but as she looked at her mother and then slid her eyes toward her father, she was suddenly struck by the gulf between her parents and herself. Had she really never noticed this before? It was as if coming to this place, this edge by the sea, had revealed that of which she had only the dimmest intimations previously. It should have been a frightening thought. But, to her surprise, more than anxiety she felt an intense, almost joyful anticipation.

THE CAVE BENEATH THE CLIFFS

MARJORIE SNOW'S GRUMPINESS continued into the evening as she complained that no one would ever find them "out here deep in the woods, deep in the fog." Lucy's father, however, seemed quite content and was focused on his sermons, somewhat distractedly trying to placate his wife with what Lucy thought of as pablum phrases, the soft cereal food for infants. For indeed Marjorie could become quite infantile when she was bored or crossed. "My dear, there is no one here yet. Fear not. They will come. We shall be sought out. Lucy shall be able to wear her tea dancing gowns and her bathing costume."

Lucy shut her eyes at the thought of the hideous bathing costume. *I'll swim in a tea gown before I wear that freakish thing*, she thought to herself.

Her father began to yawn, then her mother as well. Her father yawned again. "I declare," he said, "I believe the sea is having a soporific effect on us all."

Lucy pretended to yawn, though she was quite wide awake. *Let them all go to bed. . . .*

Her parents' room was in the back of the cottage on the first floor, while the room she had chosen was in the front on the second floor, with a window that looked straight out to sea. Lucy could not believe how bright the stars were, for the fog that had wrapped the cottage tightly for most of the day had vanished. Each pane in the window framed a half dozen silvery dots. As a seemingly endless procession of stars clambered over the horizon to the east, each pane of glass became a fragment of a puzzle. Lucy was now trying to assemble them in her mind into the constellations she had read about. Until now, her study of astronomy had all been book learning. There were no stars in Manhattan as far as she could tell. The night was too crowded with city lights and tall buildings and plumes of smoke belched from factories and furnaces. But here by the sea, the stars cut the night sharply, as if the sky and all of its constellations swooped down to touch the Earth and the sea. Darkness, Lucy realized, was the wellspring of beauty. And she could not help but wonder what beauty lay beneath the dark surface of the water for it, too, must hold unimagined treasures.

Her parents were surely asleep now. She lifted the covers from her bed and wrapped herself in a shawl, ignoring her high button shoes and her stockings draped over the chair. If the path was slippery, she'd rather be in her bare feet than those brand-new shoes with slick, unscuffed soles.

She crept down the stairs. Her eyes quickly adjusted to the darkness and in no time she was picking her way down the path. The tide was out and she was able to jump down from a ledge just a few feet above the beach shingled with rocks. The damp stones felt wonderful under her feet and she noticed that she hardly limped. Could the salt water some-how have a therapeutic effect? She felt the tendons in her ankle relax, and her foot seemed to come unbound. The sensation was so startling that she pulled up the hem of her dress and looked down. It was the same foot and yet it did not seem to turn inward nearly as much. She walked on until she saw a cleft in the rocks. A deeper darkness appeared to yawn into the night. She followed a rivulet of water that plowed a narrow path toward the cleft.

It's a cave! she thought. A real cave like in *Treasure Island*, which she had read at least half a dozen times. Or Mammoth Cave in Kentucky, which she had read about in the *Harper's Weekly* and had been dying to visit and to explore its limestone maze of tunnels. When she had suggested that they might visit this place, her mother had shrieked "*Kentucky*!" as if Lucy had suggested a trip to the moon, or perhaps Africa or the Orient.

But this was a real cave and Lucy was walking into it evenly, steadily, with no limp whatsoever. There was an almost imperceptible change in her vision, as if, within her eye, there was another that could penetrate the shadows of the cave. She could see with amazing clarity in this darkness that swirled with salty vapors from the sea.

Slabs of pink granite sloped gently from the cave

walls to where the water would flow in at high tide. She could see a line on a broad slant of rock where the tide had stopped. But then she spied something else and gasped. Three wooden pegs, tree branches really, were jammed into cracks in the rocks. Hanging from two of the branches were some girls' garments. Someone had been in this cave. She looked around cautiously. The beckoning darkness had felt so welcoming with her first steps into the cave, but now she was not so sure. What if she had accidentally intruded into the secret hideout of two close friends? They surely wouldn't be happy to find the summer pastor's daughter poking around. An overwhelming sense of loneliness suddenly swept over her. She didn't want to be excluded, not here. Not in this cave. In New York she didn't mind if girls like Elsie Ogmont or Lenora Drexel or Denise De Becque thought her odd, but here it mattered. That was the most peculiar thing of all. This was not a Fifth Avenue drawing room; this was a granite cave with a beautiful filigree of moss climbing its walls as lovely as any lace. Yet now it mattered more than ever to her that she might be thought of as peculiar. She had never felt more desolate in her life.

She came closer to the branches where a camisole hung. It was similar to the one she was wearing but almost in tatters. On the branch next to it was a petticoat in equal disrepair. There was also a velvet ribbon faded and stiff with salt, and tied to one end of it was a strangely beautiful shell, the likes of which she had never seen. It looked a bit like a scallop shell, but it was quite flat and the ribs were deeply indented. She could not resist touching it. She looked over her shoulder as if to confirm that she was alone and no one was coming. She reached out her hand slowly and noticed that her fingers were trembling.

She removed the shell and its ribbon from the branch to examine it more carefully. She gasped as she saw a strand of red hair twined through the indented ribs. Someone had worn this as a comb in her hair! She could not resist trying it in her own and loosed her hair from the night knot she always twisted it into when she went to bed. Then she ran the comb through and felt the points of the teeth scrape against her scalp. She closed her eyes. In that instant, she knew that the shell came from a place so deep that no human would ever go there. Whoever it was who had retrieved this lovely shell would be very different from those fashionable young ladies who had looked down their long patrician noses at her.

She fixed the comb so that the hair on one side was pulled back behind one ear. She only wished there was a mirror so she could see her reflection. This was a style her mother would have disapproved of as being too sophisticated, or perhaps "tartish." It occurred to her that with the rising water she might have the perfect mirror — a liquid mirror.

She walked toward the entrance of the cave in order to have the benefit of the moonlight. The water at the entrance was much higher than before. She crouched down at the edge and peered at the surface. Her face loomed up trembling on the soft undulations of the water. The reflection of stars quivered around the reflection of her face. She didn't look too sophisticated or tartish at all. Just over the crown of her head the silvery orb of the moon wobbled. Everything seemed so fragile in the liquid mirror, as if it were just a dream — a dream within a dream. Was this really happening? She touched the scallop shell again and pressed it hard into her scalp so she could feel the teeth — anything to make this moment feel real.

She knew she had to return the shell, and there was not much time, for the tide was coming in faster. She looked away from the cave to the beach. There was only a thin crescent left exposed. If she didn't leave soon, she'd have to swim back. *But I don't know how to swim.* And then she laughed out loud. For it seemed so ridiculous — of course she knew how. She just had to dare herself to try. *Soon*, she thought. *Very soon.*

She walked back into the cave and carefully replaced the shell on the stick. It was then she spied the notch like a small cubbyhole in the rocks above the three branches. There was something stuffed inside. Reaching up, she took out a tightly rolled oilskin that was about the length of one of the

Havana cigars her father sometimes smoked. She untied the string. A note fell out.

H. She has come! But not crossed. Not yet.

M

THE BREATH ON HER SKIN

A BLADE OF SUNLIGHT lay across the narrow bed, and when Lucy turned over, it fell across her face. Her eyelids flinched and she rolled back. But the sun seemed to follow her.

"Lucy! Lucy!" She heard her mother's footsteps on the stairs. "My goodness, what a sleepyhead. Do you know what time it is?"

Lucy opened one eye. "No idea." Then she forced open the other eye. She did not want to be dragged into this day. The night, what had transpired or seemed to have transpired, still stirred somewhere within her like a lingering scent. She wanted to hold on to it. But there was her mother, looking remarkably cheerful compared to last night.

"Darling, it's almost ten o'clock." She plopped herself down on the bed, narrowly avoiding sitting on Lucy's foot, the foot that now seemed as cramped as ever. Had it all been a dream? "We've had a very exciting invitation."

Lucy yawned again. "Yeah?"

"For heaven's sake don't say 'yeah.' It is so vulgar. Next thing you know, you'll be using that peculiar word the natives always say for yes."

"Ayuh!" Lucy laughed.

"That's it exactly." Marjorie Snow's eyebrows leaped high on her forehead like two small minnows. "Never mind. We didn't bring you here to learn how to speak in that odd brogue of the natives. Don't you want to know about the invitation?"

Lucy propped herself up on her elbows. "What is it?" She tried to muster some enthusiasm.

"A yachting invitation."

Lucy sat straight up. "We're going sailing? On the ocean?"

"I hardly know where else you would do it, dear. But not only that. It is with none other than the Augustus Bellamys."

"Who are the Bellamys?"

"The Bellamys, upper Fifth Avenue. Very smart people. And they have commissioned a new yacht. The biggest one ever built around here, so Elva Perry says. She brought the message this morning with a dozen fresh eggs. She is quite a dear, Mrs. Perry. Anyhow they are doing what they call a shakedown sail — working out the kinks."

"And they want us to come?"

"Yes, dear, and you especially, for I think their son will be on board." Marjorie was beaming. Lucy almost recoiled. The very thought of having to make conversation with another one of these aristocratic young men unnerved her. Small talk presented a veritable minefield of potential disasters. Her capacity to say the wrong thing, the stupid thing, was infinite in such situations. And to have Marjorie present was even worse.

The last thing she wanted to do was to embarrass or fail her mother.

"Oh, darling, I never thought it would all begin so soon. Only the day after tomorrow! I thought we were here unfashionably early, but I guess some of the

Bellamys are here early as well because of their boat — pardon me, yacht. Rumor has it, it cost almost one hundred thousand dollars. Can you imagine that?"

Lucy, however, was imagining not dollar bills but the sea — sailing on the wide-open sea.

❦ ❦ ❦

The sail had to be postponed for two days due to poor weather. But on a bright sunny Saturday morning, the Snows boarded the *Desperate Lark*.

"Ah, here you are!" Augustus Bellamy greeted them heartily as they made their way down the pier at the Heanssler boatyard. "Mrs. Snow! And young Miss Snow. Lucy, I believe? My wife is already on board with her sister and my brother-in-law. And here comes my perpetually late son, Gus."

Quick introductions were made. Gus Bellamy reached forward to shake hands with Marjorie Snow, whose voice seemed almost to trill as she took his hand in greeting.

"Gus will not actually be on the boat with us, as he is going in the steam launch with young Phineas

Heanssler to photograph *Lark*. He's got the photo bug, you know." Augustus Bellamy winked.

Thank God for the photo bug, Lucy thought. She might even be able to think of a decent question to ask about photography. However, her mother's disappointment was almost palpable.

The breeze was fresh, and within twenty minutes, the yacht, a yawl, was slicing down the eastern way between the Dog Islands. There was the pleasant creak of the mast and a shiver through the shrouds when the yacht caught the wind. As she bit the breeze, the sails puffed and the *Lark* darted ahead like the bird for which she was named. Lucy found it completely exhilarating, but her poor mother was looking quite liverish. Everything seemed to be going perfectly in this shakedown cruise. Indeed the only kink was the one in Marjorie's plans. She pressed a handkerchief to her mouth and looked longingly at the stolid little steam launch, uncharmingly named *Bongo*, that bore what she considered precious cargo — Augustus Bellamy III — with his camera set up to photograph this trial sail. The *Bongo* was being expertly piloted by Phineas Heanssler, son of Raymond Heanssler, the renowned Bar Harbor yacht builder.

The plan was to have lunch on one of the many islands that dotted the bay. For her mother's sake, Lucy decided she would make a real effort with Gus Bellamy. She had thought up at least two or three questions she might ask about photography, for she had recently seen an exhibit of William Henry Jackson's photographs of Yosemite.

"Bring her in close, Phin," Raymond Heanssler shouted over the wind. "I'm going to fall off a bit, then run her down toward the first Dog." As the steam launch swept close, Lucy caught a glimpse of Phineas Heanssler. He cut a memorable figure at the helm of the launch. His rugged profile was illuminated by a sudden blast of sunlight as he spun the wheel with authority and pulled in close to the yawl for the best shot.

"Your son will get some fine pictures, Mr. Bellamy," said Raymond Heanssler.

"I'm sure he will. Ain't she something! How she tucks into it. You've built me a fine craft, Raymond. And Phineas has a fine touch with that launch."

"Can't take too much credit. Phin did most of the design. That boy knows his way with boats and wind, and he surely knows *Lark* and how she fits to the waves."

Fits to the waves . . . what a lovely phrase, Lucy thought. She looked back over her shoulder and caught another glimpse of the young man called Phin as the steam launch laid off to port and crossed their wake.

Mr. Bellamy turned to Marjorie. "And what a sport you are, madam." He gave her a hearty slap on the back.

"Honestly, Augie, don't knock the poor woman around. I can tell she's not feeling all that well. Don't worry, Mrs. Snow. It takes some getting used to." Adelaide Bellamy was a calm, handsome woman. She had the grace and confidence that came with generations of privilege and wealth.

"Too bad the reverend couldn't come," Mr. Bellamy said. "But it looks like Lucy here was born to it. You like it, do you, Lucy?"

"Oh, yes, sir. I certainly do."

"It becomes you, it does, my dear. The sea becomes you. Puts the pink in your cheeks and that fine red hair of yours — redder than a boiled lobster! Ha-ha!" he slapped his plump thigh. There was a solid thwack as loud as the crack of the jib when they tacked. Lucy saw her mother wince.

"Boiled lobster! Honestly, Augie!" Mrs. Bellamy laughed. "You have to forgive him, Lucy. He means well. He just lacks a certain *je ne sais quoi* — eloquence?"

"You want to put in at Dog One for luncheon, Mr. Bellamy?" the captain, Cyrus Sprague, asked.

"That would suit me fine. Nice spot for a picnic."

Lucy saw her mother visibly brighten. She supposed it was not so much the prospect of lunch — for with her greenish pallor, she hardly appeared ready for food — but rather the anticipation of having Augustus Bellamy III within reach.

"Now let's see," Adelaide Bellamy said as she stepped from the dinghy onto the beach. "I think, Captain Sprague, that you can direct the crew to put our hampers over there by that boulder. Spread out the picnic rugs and bring along a few of our beach chairs as well. Over there, that looks like a fine place for you and the crew to eat."

"Yes, ma'am," Captain Sprague answered.

"No, Adelaide, I want Sprague here with us. We need to discuss what he thinks about that mizzen staysail," Mr. Bellamy said.

"With us!" Adelaide answered, hardly disguising her shock. "You mean we're going to discuss mizzen staysails all through lunch? I don't think so, Augie."

"Plenty of time to discuss mizzen staysails when we get back, Mr. Bellamy," Captain Sprague offered diplomatically, and the matter was quickly settled as Lucy thought many matters in the Bellamy family often were. Adelaide Bellamy was a formidable woman.

But again, there were still some kinks, at least from Marjorie Snow's point of view. For Gus had no interest in eating lunch and immediately scampered off to the wilder end of the island to photograph some sort of bird life. When he did return for a sandwich, he ignored his family and sat with the crew at their separate picnic grounds. Adelaide Bellamy did not seem to notice, or perhaps she did not care.

Lucy sat quietly munching a delicious crabmeat sandwich, and looked out at the seascape. Gulls hung in the sky. There was the chime of a bell buoy in the distance. It all seemed so perfect.

"Young Phineas over there" — Mr. Bellamy nodded in the direction of where the crew sat — "was really responsible for *Desperate Lark*'s design. First one he's done all on his own, though he's worked in his father's yard since the time he was just a tyke. He's an up-and-comer, that one."

Mr. Bellamy's sister-in-law, Isabel, smiled. "It's so nice when the natives find a vocation. I imagine it keeps them out of trouble."

"It's our way of investing in the island, Isabel," her sister Adelaide offered.

"A helluva investment!" August Bellamy exclaimed.

Adelaide winced. "Don't bellow, Augie!" she scolded.

The conversation made Lucy cringe. She turned her head in the direction of the picnicking men and caught Phineas looking rather intently at her, but he quickly turned the other way.

When the picnicking was finished, it was decided that Raymond Heanssler would take the ladies back in the steam launch since the breeze was kicking up. They would have to beat back against a headwind, and it would be a quicker trip to Bar Harbor on the launch. Phineas would sail on *Desperate Lark* and check the tension of the starboard shroud in a headwind.

"Might I sail back on *Desperate Lark* rather than the steam launch?" Lucy asked, eager to feel the rock of the waves.

"Why, certainly, my dear," Mr. Bellamy replied.

And, alas, once again Marjorie Snow's designs were foiled as Gus decided to accompany the ladies on the steam launch so he could get some final shots of the yacht under sail.

Lucy watched Phineas Heanssler at the wheel from her seat in the cockpit. He tipped his head up frequently to read the wind indicators, small strips of fabric that streamed from the halyards, and occasionally told a crew member to winch in one of the sheets, the lines that controlled the sails. His touch was light on the wheel.

"Would you like to take her, Miss Snow?" he asked, turning to her suddenly.

"Me?" She was amazed to be asked such a question.

"Why not?" Captain Sprague said. "Nothing to it. She's got a sweet helm on her."

The vivid, poetic language these men used to speak of yachts and the sea enchanted Lucy, and watching them was even more magical. Phineas seemed to barely touch the wheel; it was as if he were guiding the craft by his thoughts alone. He was not at first glance what one would call hand-some, but he was so different looking from any of the young men she had met in New York. He was not what her father called "well barbered." His reddish blond hair curled down over the frayed collar of his tan shirt. On his belt was a slim holster with a knife. She supposed it must be some equipment for cut-ting lines on the yacht. His features were irregular and far from perfect. Yet his eyes were a blue the likes of which she had never seen, and his eye-brows were bleached almost white by the sea. But it was his hands that intrigued Lucy. They were long and elegant and might have been those of a pianist rather than a shipbuilder, and yet they were rough. She saw thick calluses on his right hand, and his nails were not only unpolished but showed a bit of grime. He stood steady in his sea boots, which bunched up the cuffs of his trousers to just below his knees.

Had he ever worn a tie? Lucy wondered. Did he own a frock coat? A straw boater hat, so fashionable these days in the summer? She watched his movements, which seemed at one with the yacht's, so balanced and steady as he leaned into the gusts and braced himself against the swells beneath the keel — but had he ever danced a waltz?

He turned to her now. "Come on, give it a try. I know you got your sea legs. I saw how you were standing there by the rail not even touching it when we came through that chop a bit ago. And when we heeled — you just leaned into it natural as can be." He smiled. "Most girls start screeching like banshees when a yacht heels a bit."

"Well, I'll try, but I don't want to be the one to wreck the Bellamys' brand-new yacht."

"Doncha worry," Captain Sprague said. "Give *Lark* a woman's touch."

"I'll stand right behind you," Phineas said. "If you get nervous, just tell me and I'll take over."

But Lucy did not get nervous. The moment she touched the wheel, she knew exactly what to do. And she barely held the lovely mahogany circle. She let the wheel glide through her hands like a silk ribbon. There was no need to grip it. She wasn't aware of steering at all. It was as if she was in a complete and perfect communion with the yacht, the wind, and the sea. From the keel that sliced through the water to the vast expanses of snowy white sails held by slender spars and taut halyards, to the lisp of the seas as they parted to make way for this lovely craft, she sensed a beautiful conspiracy of sorts — a conspiracy of wind and water, stick and string, canvas and shroud. A calm stole through her. Here was something created by man that had achieved a perfect balance in this universe. Behind her stood the young man who had built this ship.

"What's it like to build a yacht?" Lucy asked. "I mean, how do you imagine the beautiful lines? The breezes her sails must catch?"

Phineas was silent for a minute. "You know, no one ever asked me about shipbuilding and designing in quite that way. But, yes, I do dream about it — her lines, how she puts her shoulder to a wave, the water streaming by her keel. I dream about it all."

Lucy leaned a bit as she turned the wheel just ever so slightly to come off the wind a degree.

"Look at that!" Captain Sprague said as he watched Lucy. "She was about to get headed by the shift and she came off just a fraction. You'd think she's been doing this all her life."

"Indeed." Phineas paused. "All her life." The fine hairs on the back of her neck rose, for she could actually feel Phineas Heanssler's breath on her skin as he spoke.

THE LAWS OF SALT

H. She has come! But not crossed.
Not yet.
M

Hannah whispered the words to herself. It seemed impossible, yet there were three carved mer infants on the sea chest that May had discovered hidden in the lighthouse. But more than that was the inexplicable, shadowy space they sometimes felt beside them as they swam. Neither Hannah nor May had spoken of the spaces until long after they met, but then they speculated endlessly on how nothingness could have such a presence. "At first," May said, "I thought it was our parents, but now that there is just one, I think it must be our sister, because one space certainly disappeared when we met." Hannah nodded in agreement, for she had experienced the same sensation when she had finally met May.

Hannah was waiting for May when she returned to the cave. She'd taken down the scallop shell and was looking at it, when she heard May swimming through the entrance. She turned to greet her as her sister pulled herself up onto the slope of granite rock. "I told you I'll show you where to get one of those scallops!" May Plum said as Hannah came to the edge where the tide lapped onto the rock. She saw the serious look on Hannah's face. "What catastrophe has beset the Hawley household now?" May asked as she lifted herself onto the rock and let her tail rest in the water.

"No catastrophe," Hannah replied. She was still studying the scallop shell. "Just the usual confusion."

"Did you read my note?"

"Yes!" Hannah said with her eyes still on the scallop.

"She's here. She came. It's like we always thought."

Hannah looked up now and flashed a broad smile. "It's more than we thought." Her voice had a conspiratorial tone.

"What are you talking about?"

"May, she's been here," Hannah exclaimed with unbridled excitement.

"Here?" May asked, slightly bewildered.

"Yes, here, right here! In this cave! Look at your comb!"

Hannah held out the scallop with the pale strand of hair laced between the tines. May gasped.

"That's certainly not my hair," Hannah said with a smile that just bordered on being smug. Although both Hannah and May had red hair, Hannah's was a much brighter red. May joked that her own was as rusty as a bag of old nails. But this strand of hair was the color of pale fire, more gold than red.

"Well, this makes sense in a way," May said as she glanced around the cave, looking for other evidence.

"What do you mean?" Hannah asked.

"She's the preacher's daughter."

"The summer preacher?" Hannah asked. "Chapel by the Sea?"

"Yes, the old fellow, the bishop, fell ill. The new preacher and his family are staying in the rectory."

May tipped her head up and pointed toward the rock ceiling of the cave. "She must have gotten down the cliffs by the rectory cottage."

Hannah stared at May. "Do you think she . . . swam?"

"No, I'm sure she hasn't crossed over," May replied confidently.

Hannah rolled her eyes. "You're always so sure about things. Nobody goes down that cliff path. It's treacherous."

"Well, she did. You have the proof. Her hair is in the comb," May said. "We have to get out of here. Look, the tide's ebbing. She might come."

"What's wrong with that? Don't you want to meet her?" Hannah smiled. "Or are you 'fraid she's too fine for us?"

May stared at Hannah. It still gave her a thrill to see her own green eyes looking back at her. It was hard to believe that, just a year earlier, she had felt so alone. "No, Hannah, we can't. Not yet."

Hannah crossed her arms and regarded her sister. "I don't understand. She's our sister, May." She paused. "Our family!"

"I knew you were one —" It sounded so cold the way May said it, but she could not help herself. Hannah had to understand. "I couldn't just come up to you. I had to wait for you to cross."

The color rose in Hannah's cheeks. She had dropped her legs over the edge into the water and the mysterious transformation began fusing them into a tail. She stroked the glittering scales. There was a truth in what May had just said that she did not want to admit. "I hate it when you call her 'one.' We're sisters. I can't see how you justify this."

"I don't justify it." May leaned forward and put her hand softly on Hannah's. "It's not me."

"Then what is it?"

"The Laws of Salt."

Hannah winced at the four innocent-seeming words. She had never heard May say them before,

but someone else had. Stannish Whitman Wheeler —
America's foremost portrait painter and Hannah
Albury's secret beau, who once upon a time had
been a mer. No longer, however. For the Laws of Salt
were harsh, and after a time, one could never turn
back. One had to choose between two worlds. May
might think she understood the Laws of Salt, but she
did not know them in the painful way that Hannah
knew them.

TO PLEASE HERSELF

HE DREAMS OF SHIPS. It was such a lovely notion. Lucy smiled to herself as she tried to imagine what Eldon Drexel dreamed of. *Coffers?* Despite her best efforts to forget him, Phineas Heanssler continued to hover around the edges of her mind all week. She almost cowered when she thought of what her mother would say about all this. Not that anything had happened. Nothing would happen. He was an islander, a "native," as Isabel Schuyler had so kindly pointed out. And though Lucy was not an heiress, she was a reverend's daughter, a reverend who someday soon might become the bishop of New York.

Yet, she couldn't help but wish Phineas hadn't insisted on calling her Miss Snow. To him, she was probably just another rich summer person who spent the season flitting between parties and sailing trips. He most likely lumped her together with all the other summer people, just as Isabel Schuyler lumped all the natives together.

Nevertheless, when she went into the village, she kept hoping for a glimpse of him, even though she knew he must spend all his time at the ship-yard. She even had, on occasion, taken a roundabout route to the Quoddy Club, where she was diligently taking tennis lessons, in order to walk by the yard. She wasn't sure if she dared to actually enter the yard itself. Summer people did not wander around there unless they were like the Bellamys, discussing plans for their yacht. Too bad she didn't have the money to order one; then Phineas Heanssler could dream about *her* ship! And maybe even dream of her.

However, it was not just Phineas and the lure of the boatyard that occupied her thoughts. It was the cave. She went when she could, hoping to find some-thing, or perhaps someone — the writer of the mysterious note. She was careful to go at low or mid tide; the power of the sea frightened but at the same time drew her near. She could see the tidal currents just off the beach, swirling eddies and once a riptide that had torn loose a dinghy from the harbor around the corner.

On calm nights, she would dip her feet in. Her bad foot had improved so much that she barely limped, so she'd agreed to take tennis lessons, which pleased her mother immensely but gave Lucy little joy.

As she returned from her tennis lesson one morning, she began her circuitous route but when she rounded a corner, she nearly crashed into Phineas coming the other way.

"Oh!" she said. A feeling of absolute glee flooded through her. *It's him!*

There he was, not two feet from her — the red hair, the sparkling blue eyes that put the sky to shame even on this bright day.

"My apologies, Miss Snow," he said, glancing around. "I didn't mean to run you down." He didn't say this with a smile, or any trace of humor.

"Oh . . . oh. No. N-n-o. It's fine," she stuttered.

Why was he speaking to her like this? They were both quickly sinking into a swamp of incoherence. She had to do something to save the situation. She'd had no trouble speaking to him before. Why weren't the words coming to her now? Had she imagined everything that had happened on the *Lark*?

"I had a very nice time sailing that day." She paused. "With the Bellamys." She dared herself to say it: "And with you."

"With me?" he said slowly.

"Yes. I enjoyed listening to you talk about your shipbuilding." A woman she recognized from the Quoddy Club walked past them and shot Lucy a strange look. She saw Phin flinch and drop his gaze. Lucy felt her cheeks start to burn, but something compelled her to continue. "You're the first person I've met up here that has anything interesting to say."

Phin raised his eyebrows. "Are you mocking me, Miss Snow?"

Lucy's stomach plummeted. "No, of course not." Was she destined always to say the wrong thing?

"Where are you going?" he asked quickly, as if he feared his voice might give out. Then he looked at the racket she was carrying and blushed. "Kind of a foolish question. I guess you're playing tennis."

"Hardly," Lucy said. She wanted to shout, *I am not a summer person!* The last thing she wanted to look like was a lifetime member of the Quoddy Club. "I think it's an incredibly stupid game," she said almost breathlessly.

"I'm not sure I agree," Phineas said.

Oh God, did I offend him? Is he a great champion tennis player? Although she didn't believe natives played tennis.

"It's not stupid?"

"It is, but there's a stupider game." He smiled for the first time. "Golf." He shook his head. "I'd rather watch paint dry. In fact, I *do* watch paint dry down in the yard."

"Where are you going?" she asked, feeling herself relax.

"To the boatyard." He hesitated.

"It must be an interesting place to work."

"It is. . . . I mean, if you like sawdust and varnish, that is." The way he pronounced *varnish* with his Maine accent almost sounded like *vanish* to Lucy's ears.

"Those are good smells, I would think," she replied.

"Would you like to come with me?" He shrugged his shoulders. "You can see it and smell it for yourself." He laughed self-consciously.

Lucy hesitated. She could only imagine what would happen if they were spotted. The Bar Harbor summer residents might dress more casually than their New York counterparts, but they were decidedly old-fashioned when it came to rules of decorum. Walking with a boy unchaperoned was frowned upon. Walking with a *local* boy could cause a real scandal. But as she thought about the alternative, an afternoon at the Quoddy Club, the decision became clear. "Thank you. I would really like to see the boatyard."

"Well, follow me," he replied.

She pulled down her straw sun hat a bit farther to shade her face and fell into step beside him. He had long legs and he was walking quickly. She dipped her chin a bit and, keeping her eyes down, smiled to herself as she spotted his sea boots. There was something delicious about walking with someone who'd look so wonderfully out of place in the Ogmonts' drawing room.

Lucy loved the Heanssler yard the moment she set foot inside. Phineas took her on an extensive tour, beginning with the shed where the shipwrights worked. She loved the smell of the wood and the varnish, and the sounds of the caulking hammers pressing oakum between the planks to make a craft watertight. The boatyard was an orderly little universe in which the tasks of building a fine, swift craft assumed the beauty and sanctity that was as holy as any church ritual.

Phin led her up the stairs to the sail loft, where both men and women cut and sewed the long strips of canvas for the sails. Most fascinating of all, however, was the drafting room, where Phineas and his father worked, drawing the lines of the hulls and the sail plans. It seemed to Lucy that the business of boatbuilding, although mysterious, was one of the most honest endeavors in the world.

Then he led her into a smaller room where, against the wall, were models of every boat they had ever designed, from coastal fishing boats to steamers to the brilliant New York Yacht Club "one-design" boats and the large sleek yachts like the Bellamys'. She walked up to one that was a deep reddish color. "What kind of wood is it?" she asked.

Phin glanced at the model. "Pine, mostly. It's soft and easy to work. That's an old model. Pine turns red over time." He turned to face Lucy. "Kind of like your hair color, isn't it?"

The sudden intensity of his gaze made her shiver. "I'm not that old," Lucy said, trying to hide her nervousness. "This was carved in 1870!" She laughed. "So how does the model help you?" It was amazing to Lucy that they were both conversing so easily now. Something about the boatyard seemed to put them both at ease.

Phin walked over toward her and picked up the model. "First, we make a preliminary sketch, on a small scale, and try to predict all the values, like weight, flotation, center of mass. Then I carve a study model." He replaced the model on the shelf and patted the holster on his belt. "Though not this one; 1870 is a bit before my time as well."

"But where does the shape begin?" Lucy asked, running her hand along another nearby model.

"Up here." Phin tapped his head. "It's like you said. I dream it." A thrill ran through her. She couldn't believe he had remembered her words from that day.

"Just dream? Is that all it takes?" she asked.

"No. There's plenty of math. We have to do a lot of calculations after we draw the lines."

"It sounds a good deal more complicated than tennis."

"It's just what I do. Born to do, I guess you could say."

"Born to do," Lucy murmured. What exactly was *she* born to do? For some reason she thought of the cave. "I'd better be on my way. My mother will be worried." The anxieties she had so willfully dispatched twenty minutes before suddenly rushed through her. What if her mother saw her leaving the boat-yard? What excuse could she make up? She twirled the tennis racket in her hand.

"Come back anytime, Miss Snow," Phin said, returning to his formal demeanor. "I'll show you out."

Say when. Don't be so vague! she wanted to scream. She felt utterly stupid standing there, twirl-ing the tennis racket. When it clattered to the floor, she blushed to her roots. "I told you I couldn't play."

"I thought you were just standing there, not playing."

"You're right." She laughed.

"Hey, listen. Don't take up golf, all right?"

"You can count on it," Lucy replied as she began to walk away.

"Uh . . . hey." His voice seemed to break. She turned around and saw him looking down and scuff-ing the floor with the toes of his sea boots. "Can I count on seeing you again?" He didn't look up.

Lucy inhaled sharply. "You mean it?"

"Ayuh. Wouldn't have said it if I didn't." He was

still looking down, dragging the toe of a boot in small circles.

"I would be really happy to see you again."

He lifted his head now and a smile broke across his face. "You're welcome anytime."

Lucy was nearly giddy by the time she came up the path to the cottage.

But then she heard her mother's voice. It was high pitched, as if she were in a nervous state about something. The words floating out of the open windows of the cottage were quite distinct.

"Oh, Stephen — the Bellamys' summer ball! You know I was so worried when we went on that sail, because Lucy and Gus barely exchanged a word. He was so absorbed with his photography. But then he came up to me at the club to deliver the invitation. It's for all of us, of course. And it's white tie! It's in celebration of — oh, what do they call it — the longest day —"

"The solstice."

"Yes, that's the word. Oh, dear, sometimes I really wish you could put your clerics aside. You'd look so handsome in white tie, but Lucy will look stunning in that green faille that Mrs. Simpson made up for her. You know, with her eyes."

Lucy couldn't stand to hear another word. Balls, gowns — it was the exact opposite of the boatyard she had just visited — that honest place. The thought of having to make forced conversation with those superficial people made her ill.

She had until now confined her visits to the cave to nighttime. It was late afternoon, but it seemed even later, as if a premature twilight had thickened the air and cast a bluish light through the woods. Her parents would expect her home soon. But she simply could not stand talking about the Bellamy ball.

The tide was coming in when she got to the small crescent of beach. She knew she could not stay long. She only needed to stay a bit, just long enough to collect her wits. The cave always seemed to soothe her.

However, on this late afternoon, it would not calm her. At least not at first. There had seemed to be such a presence there, and yet at the same time a haunting emptiness.

It was not always possible for Lucy to come at the same time, for the tides were constantly changing. It had now been two weeks since their arrival on the island, and low tide was pushed back to the late morning hours. To come in the secret of the night had been impossible because that was high tide. She had missed the place dearly, and now, as she walked the beach, she had to pull up the hem of her dress to step carefully from rock to rock.

The green shadows of the cave stretched out to welcome her. She loved how the moss grew on the granite walls. Like delicate embroidery it fanned out across the pinkish stone, and she had tried to capture its fineness in her painting. On her last visit she had brought two bottles of colored ink, a small tablet of drawing paper, and two brushes, and had made a watercolor sketch of the cave. Then, after it dried, she had carefully rolled it into the oilskin with the note. She always checked the little cleft in the rock where she had found the note and was anxious to see if there was any sign that her painting had been discovered. A little glimmering crystal flake drifted to the ground as she unrolled the oilskin. But there was nothing new and the drawing was still in place, perhaps a little crumpled at its edge. She felt a deep twinge of disappointment. Outside she heard the shuddering hoot of an owl that seemed to echo her own chagrin.

She tried to imagine Phineas's face from earlier in the afternoon, but it kept slipping away from her, like a reflection on water suddenly splintered by a disturbance on the surface. The water was lapping over the edge of the rocks. If she stayed much longer, she would have to wade home.

Lucy unlaced her shoes, peeled off her stockings, and dipped her feet in the shallow pool of water. It always felt lovely and indeed it seemed to have helped her foot. She could probably dance just fine. But she didn't want to dance. She had no interest in being paraded in front of her mother's "suitable young men" like a thoroughbred at auction. *I want to swim*, she thought.

She looked down at the water, and her eyes widened. There was a luminescence in the pool, issuing from her feet. She wriggled her toes, and the water swirled with a shimmering iridescence. Lucy pulled one foot out of the water and ran her fingertips over the skin. Skin? It was now almost translucent, and just beneath the surface, tiny ovals were glinting softly. When she removed her hand, two or three crystals that seemed the shape of teardrops were glittering on her fingertips. "*What in the world?*" she whispered. She remembered the crystal that had drifted down from the oilskin, to which she had paid no heed, and scrambled back to search for it on the rock beneath the cleft. But it was impossible to find, for the rock itself was chinked with mica chips and streaked with quartz.

The tide was rising faster. She knew she had to get back quickly. Picking up her shoes and stockings, she waded out of the cave, mesmerized by the radiant swirls that marked her passage through the now knee-deep water. She sensed the beginnings of a secret mutiny in her heart as the tide pulled on her ankles and the water gently licked her skin.

She turned just before she climbed on to the higher ground. There was a fading wake behind her that was slowly dissolving. "I'll be back," she whispered. "I'll be back."

"OUR KIND"

"OH, LUCY, where on earth have you been?" her mother exclaimed as she walked in the door. "So much has happened!"

Though heavily corseted, Marjorie Snow seemed to be almost visibly bursting at the seams of her dress. She did not even wait for Lucy to answer the question and did not seem to notice the splashes of seawater on Lucy's dress despite Lucy's attempts to tuck it up. Marjorie rushed toward her daughter, waving the cream-colored invitation to the Bellamy ball.

"First this — delivered by Gus at the Quoddy Club. We are all invited, of course. And then, just minutes ago, an invitation arrived from the Hawleys for a Fourth of July croquet tournament and picnic. I mean, this is really something. The picnic is an affair that the smart set always shows up for." *Smart* had quickly become Marjorie Snow's favorite word since arriving in Bar Harbor.

"There are rumors that some titled people are arriving soon and that they'll be attending these events as well."

"Titled people? Like counts and lords?" A note of fear crept into Lucy's voice. She couldn't speak to a banker without making a fool out of herself and could only imagine what would happen to her in the presence of a count.

The funny muscle near Marjorie's eye flinched. "Of course that means counts and lords. Sometimes you can be so obtuse." Marjorie shook her head in mild despair.

"It's nothing to sneer at, Lucy," continued her father. "These titled people, English lords and the like, have wonderful connections. You should really make an effort to form an acquaintance."

"But why would an English lord want to celebrate the Fourth of July?" Lucy asked. "They lost."

Her father chuckled. "Now, that is witty!"

"Witty!" Marjorie almost screeched the word. "Wit gets you nowhere, Stephen! We don't need witty. Look how our dear Lucy has blossomed. Her limp is practically gone since she arrived."

The reverend turned to his daughter. "I completely agree. Never lovelier. But 'wit,' as your mother calls it, will do nothing but distract from your other charms."

Her mother inhaled sharply, and Lucy could hear the stays of her corset emit a small crack. "I'll tell you who's *witty*!" her mother said.

"Who?" Lucy asked tentatively.

"That Green girl."

"Green girl?" Lucy was baffled.

"Remember that governess, Miss Burnham, whom we met on the steamship coming here?"

"You mean the one you thought we'd never see again?"

"Yes, I did see her in town when I went for tea with Mrs. Allen at the Abenaki Club. This Miss Burham was there with two of her charges. The two Green girls. One was just ten years old or so, but the other was around your age. . . ."

"What did she say that was so witty?"

"Well, you know they have a rocking horse in the lobby for the youngsters? There was a rather chubby little boy riding it, and the older girl made some remark about Theodore Roosevelt and the charge up San Juan Hill. I can't remember what, exactly, but people laughed."

"What's wrong with that, Mother?"

"Oh . . . oh . . . ." Marjorie wiggled her fingers in the air as if again she was searching for the right words. "It was . . . was, you know, an *intellectual* type of humor. Apparently, this older Green girl attends Radcliffe!"

"The women's college in Cambridge?"

"Indeed!" the reverend scoffed. He was now behind a newspaper. "Women wanted to breach the walls of Harvard. Never a good idea. So a college was made next door for them. The women then were a bit like Teddy Roosevelt — charging up San Juan Hill — just Harvard instead." This time her father did not laugh but buried himself deeper in the newspaper he was reading. Marjorie gave a deep sigh and there were a few more creaks from her corset as if in protest of her daughter's obtuseness.

"I think this Miss Green sounds very interesting. I'd like to meet her." Lucy almost surprised herself with this forthright declaration. Never before would she have voiced something that was so distinctly contrary to her parents' wishes, but something was changing in her. Miss Green sounded interesting, just as Phineas Heanssler was interesting in a way that Lenora Drexel or that whole lot in New York were not.

"You won't." The voice swirled up from behind the newspaper with the pipe smoke.

"Why not?" There she had done it again, spoken with a boldness that took her aback. It just seemed to sneak up on her.

"Stephen?" her mother said feebly.

There was the soft sound of the newspaper being folded. Stephen Snow set it down on the table beside him and removed the pipe from his mouth.

"Lucy dear." The word *dear* seemed out of place, for there was a stony look in her father's eyes. A coldness in his voice. "This is an island. It is a very small world — a microcosm, if you will, of society. Things were simpler for us in New York. I was the shepherd of a small downtown flock, and while St. Luke's was, you can be assured, highly regarded, it was not —"

"In the thick." Marjorie Snow lassoed these three words as deftly as a cowboy running down a stray from the herd.

"Thank you, my dear."

"Now we are — to use your mother's words — in the thick. Believe me, I have never worked so hard on my sermons. We're in a different league now. Yesterday, I looked out into the congregation and I saw titans there — three of them in the first two pews — Van Wyck, the steel magnate from Pennsylvania, old Astor, and a Rockefeller." He leaned forward. "So you ask why can you not meet with this young Jewess? I'm sure she is a perfectly fine girl. Maybe even a lovely girl." Marjorie frowned. "Certainly an intelligent girl — most Jews are very intelligent. But they are Jews. Not our kind."

Not our kind. The words rang in Lucy's head like dolorous chimes. *What is my kind?* she thought as she recalled the swirling iridescence that had radiated from her feet. She slipped her hand into the pocket of the dress where she had tucked the glittering crystals she had rubbed from her skin.

There was one thing of which Lucy was certain. She was not *their* kind.

11

BELLEMERE

AN ARBOR ENCRUSTED with trailing ivy and studded with gardenias had been erected in the arched entrance to the ballroom, and an orchestra brought up from Boston struck up the first notes of a waltz. The walls were painted with murals celebrating the unmatched rugged beauty of coastal Maine — sweeping vistas of seascapes and rockbound shores.

"Now, dear boy, give me the players list." A young gentleman with slicked-back hair and wearing an elegantly tailored frock coat stood next to another man, who was slightly older and less elaborately dressed.

"Well, first of all, Your Grace, you must understand that this is not Newport, despite all this," the older man said as he waved a hand at the elaborate floral archway they were standing beneath. "Although it is rumored that a student of Audubon's painted the murals."

"I agree, it is hardly Newport," the Duke of Crompton replied, looking about. "Not a touch of marble, and all these cottages mostly shingled on the outside and wood inside."

"You are, I imagine, referring to the Vanderbilts' marble cottage, the Breakers, in Newport?"

"Yes, I was there a week ago for the Rose Ball. That's why I was late arriving in Bar Harbor. But shingles. Aren't they fearful of fire?"

"Possibly, but you know it's a different crowd here. Make no mistake, the Bellamys most likely can match the Vanderbilts dime for dime. The Forbes certainly can."

"Yes, but she's engaged." He sighed somewhat mournfully. "What's her name? Melinda?"

"Matilda. She's engaged to the Earl of Lyford. But you see the difference here is, as they say, 'high thinking and plain living.'"

"It is all rather plain, isn't it?" The duke cast his

eyes about. "But not her." His voice betrayed the first hint of enthusiasm he'd shown all evening.

"Who?" the older gentleman asked.

"That tall redheaded girl over there. She just came in with her parents."

"Ah, yes, the preacher's daughter."

"Preacher's daughter? Oh, dear," he replied, barely concealing a shudder.

"Don't be too dismissive, Your Grace. It's rumored that the Reverend Snow is slated to become the next bishop of New York, and his wife has deep connections in Baltimore."

"Really?" The duke sighed. "Well, there is no one else who can compare with her in the room." He swiveled his head about. "I mean, really, most of them are quite plain and many are a tad chubby. Oh, except that one — absolute scarecrow!" He scanned the room again for the auburn-haired beauty.

What would Mama say to a preacher's daughter — but possibly a wealthy one? He would have to find out. Though the duke loathed leaving Newport, the best girls had been picked off already. The problem here was, well, exactly what had already been said. High thinking and plain living. It was impossible to see who was worth the effort. It was all just too plain, so very plain. It was a far cry from the London crushes last season with all those lovely, well-bred girls in their Parisian gowns. But, sadly, all their dresses were bought on credit, and their dainty evening purses were empty. If he was to have any chance of saving the Crompton estate, he'd have to look on this side of the pond.

❧ ❧ ❧

"They call this a cottage, Mother?" Lucy asked, tipping her head up to scan the grand ballroom of Bellemere, the Bellamy estate. "These murals are so beautiful. Look how that painter captured the sea. Imagine living in the midst of this art."

"Yes, dear, they do call it a cottage. It's quite understated here compared to Newport. Much *older* money."

Lucy had never been to Newport, Rhode Island, another summer enclave, but it was true that there was not the gilt-encrusted opulence of some of the

New York Fifth Avenue mansions. But why anyone would call this a cottage defied imagination.

"In Newport," her mother whispered, "the men servants are often bewigged in the style of the English footmen." She paused. "I am told — not that I have ever attended such an affair." She spoke with a slightly simpering humility.

There was a rustle behind them, and they turned to see people parting as the hostess cut through the throngs of men and women, nodding and uttering clipped greetings.

In her bright blue moiré silk dress, Adelaide Bellamy appeared like a fine yacht as she tacked across the ballroom.

"Ah, just the people I wanted to see. The dear Snows!" she exclaimed. Lucy could almost feel her mother swelling with pride. "And, Lucy, don't you look glorious in that sea-green silk faille and lace. My goodness, it becomes you. And your hair! Did you go to Harriet Beatty in the village?"

"No, my mother did it." Lucy paused slightly. "She's very good with hair."

Lucy saw the color drain from her mother's face

and realized she had said the wrong thing. Adelaide Bellamy leaned forward.

"My dear, I am sure this is the least of your mother's talents." Her nose, which Lucy realized was quite monumental, seemed to close the space between them. "Now I want to introduce you since simply everyone has arrived for the season. Can't guarantee the reverend that they all show up in church every Sunday. But come along."

She slipped her arm through Marjorie Snow's and began to pilot her across the room with Lucy and her father in their wake. Elaborate epergnes spilled with orchids from the Bellamy greenhouses, the band struck up a mazurka, and several young couples took to the floor in the first dance of the evening. Some worn beauties coerced their husbands onto the floor. On the side of the great room was a row of gilt chairs where a dozen decidedly ancient people sat. Two old ladies were in wheelchairs and gave the appearance of withered babies tucked in with mohair blankets.

"My twin aunties," Mrs. Bellamy said. "Big Adelaide and Auntie Barbara."

"You can call me Bobby," a voice creaked from the bloodless lips that seemed stitched like a short seam. She took Marjorie's hand in her own puffy one, which had a filigree of blue veins.

"Lovely to meet you." Marjorie turned slightly and began to extend her hand to Big Adelaide.

"She can't speak! Not a blessed word!" Bobby said with surprising vigor, then emitted a high cackling noise.

Lucy suddenly felt a hand on her elbow.

"Hello, Lucy." It was Gus Bellamy.

"There you are, Gus," his mother said. "I was just making the rounds with the Snows."

"Yes, I can see, but I think now that she has met the aunties, Lucy can perhaps move on to . . . the younger generation."

Marjorie was beaming. "Oh, yes. I'm sure Lucy would be interested in meeting some of the other young folk. She has met several at the Quoddy Club, but more have arrived now . . . for . . ." — she hesitated — "the season." She spoke the last words with a shadow of uncertainty as if perhaps she did not have the right to use the word *season*, that it was something reserved only for people like the Bellamys, the Van Wycks, the Astors, and the other old-money families who had come to this island for generations.

Lucy looked about as Gus guided her to the other side of the room.

"You've been coming here for a long time?" Lucy asked.

"All my life. And my father has been coming all his life. My mother met my father here. She's a Van Wyck by birth and came here from the time she was a little girl. That is how it is." There was a weariness in his voice. "And always has been. There are the Van Wycks with their rather prominent noses and an athleticism to match. My mother is a terrific tennis player. Then my father's family, the Bellamys, known for their exuberance for real estate."

"And what about the other families — what are their distinguishing traits?" Lucy asked. She felt at ease with Gus and his straightforward speech.

"Well, take the Benedicts. They're into mining — quite lucrative, needless to say, but" — he lowered his voice and leaned closer to Lucy — "streaks of insanity have afflicted them in alternating generations. And of course there's the Hawleys from Boston, over there across the room. Made their fortunes in the China trade and also have a tincture of madness, especially in the eldest daughter, Lila. They say she's visiting abroad or something, but rumor has it she's in a loony bin." He sighed. "I am not as familiar with the hallmarks of the other Boston families, the Peabodys, the Forbeses, and the Cabots. But we're all the same — coming together, mingling bloodlines, converging fortunes." His ennui was so thick as to be almost palpable.

"You don't like it?"

"It really isn't a question of like. It's all I know and ever have known." He shook his head and smiled. "I'm sure I'm boring you with my genealogy lesson."

"Not at all," Lucy replied. "It's all new to me."

"So what are your initial observations?"

They had wandered out onto a veranda. There were just a few people, mostly young, in the long blue twilight of the summer evening. It was almost ten but not quite dark enough for the stars to sparkle.

She stopped and looked about. She saw another prominent nose — a Van Wyck, no doubt — and recalled the words of Dr. Forsythe at the Museum of Natural History: "I don't think of them so much as families but tribes."

"Tribes?" Gus said, as if trying the word for the first time. "How curious. But, yes, I see what you mean — it is quite tribal." He looked at her quizzically. "You're a rather deep thinker, I believe."

"Is that bad?" Lucy stepped back slightly and looked at him with a level gaze.

"Hardly. It's wonderfully refreshing." He took a deep breath. "Let me warn you, however."

"Have I transgressed?" She smiled, despite her sudden nervousness.

"Not at all. But I think you are wise enough to understand when I say that you could become — well, how should I put it? A project for my mother."

"A project?"

"Let me speak plainly. My mother senses you are bright. She knows your mother has ambitions."

Lucy felt herself redden. "Is my mother that transparent?"

"Now don't worry!" He touched her shoulder lightly in a brotherly manner. "Mother is afflicted with a bad case of the Lady Bountifuls. She and her friends are constantly organizing benefits for orphanages and homeless young women, dragging the hems of their skirts through the swill and ditchwater of the poorest sections of New York."

"But I am not an orphan, nor do I live in swill," Lucy said, unable to suppress the twinge of irritation in her voice. "I am not in need of salvation. After all, my father is an Episcopal minister."

"Ah, but that is just the point. My mother does not restrict herself to the obviously afflicted."

"In what way am I afflicted?" Lucy asked.

"You're bright. You're very pretty, but you have no money."

Lucy paled. "That's rather coarse, Mr. Bellamy."

He shrugged. "It's the truth and there are rumors that your father might be the next bishop of New York."

"Mr. Bellamy!" Lucy had never heard anyone at such a gathering speak so forthrightly. There was none of that glibness that she had found so detestable in New York, and yet this, too, set her at a loss for words.

"Don't be shocked. We might be the only two people in this room capable of speaking the truth. Without money, the possibilities of a match are limited. So they must find someone for you — good stock and with some money but not too much money." He stopped and cocked his head a bit. "Like me. I have too much money. Because then you might be considered a fortune hunter."

"I am not!" Lucy fumed. How could she ever be considered a fortune hunter? Had she unwittingly done something, said something, to hint at such base instincts? Or — a dreadful thought coursed through her. Had her parents done something?

"Of course you're not."

"And I would never — I mean — I wouldn't." She had begun to stammer.

"Lucy, my dear. You need not explain. You are not attracted to me. No need for apology. And, while I think you're quite lovely, I have another sweetheart."

"You do?"

"Yes, and she is heartily disapproved of by my parents," he said with barely concealed frustration.

"Is she here?"

"She's on the island but not here at Bellemere."

"Who is she?" Lucy asked, suddenly curious.

"Her name is Anna Green."

Lucy gasped. "Anna Green the . . . the . . ."

"Jewess. Yes, she is Jewish. And I met her here on the island last summer. Her family began coming here a few years back. They found the climate agreeable for Mrs. Green. At least, the weather and sea breezes were suitable, not the climate. The climate is not good for Jews. We met just last summer for the first time. You are so right when you say the island is tribal."

"I'm sorry for you."

"Well, I'm sorry for you."

"Why? Because your mother wants to make a project of me? Whom does she have in mind as the perfect not-too-rich-but-of-good-stock match for a would-be bishop's daughter?"

"That gent over there." He nodded toward a thin young man with sandy-colored hair.

"He looks perfectly decent, I suppose."

"He is perfectly decent. A distant cousin from the poor branch of the Benedicts. Not very bright, however, and not for you."

"So," Lucy continued, smiling, "you feel that you know the sort of man for me, I take it?"

"Not the sort, but specifically — Phineas Heanssler." Lucy felt herself sway a bit. Gus grinned and grabbed her elbow. "Steady there, old girl."

"I'm sure you are mistaken," Lucy said, removing her arm from his grip. "Please put this out of your mind. It's ridiculous. Utterly ridiculous."

Gus raised his eyebrows. "I have the pictures."

"What pictures?" Lucy's eyes flashed with anxiety.

"From when you were on *Desperate Lark*."

"But Phineas wasn't on the yacht. He was with you — until we came back, and then you were taking the ladies back to shore on the steam launch."

"He caught sight of you from the steam launch when we were sailing out to the Dog Islands. I could tell he was mesmerized. He asked me when we came up close for a series of shots if I could take one of you. I teased him a bit about it and promised I would make a copy for him. Then when he got on board — well, you should see the pictures. He's hardly tending to the yacht at all. Although I have to say, you did a fine job at the helm."

"Why didn't your parents invite him to this party?"

He coughed a bit before answering. The question seemed to have thrown him slightly. "As you said. It's all very tribal. Anna Green and Phineas Heanssler are not our tribe," he said bitterly.

Our kind, Lucy thought.

"Thank you, Gus. Thank you for speaking so . . . honestly!" She turned and went back into the ballroom.

"Oh, there you are, my dear!" Lucy's mother bustled up to her with a brittle sparkle in her eyes. "Come here. I want to introduce you to two lovely young gentlemen. This is James Benedict and this is Percy Wilgrew, the Duke of Crompton. Gentlemen, may I present my daughter, Lucy. We are here for the season." This time, the word *season* resonated with confidence.

The duke picked up Lucy's hand and kissed it lightly. She could smell the sweet oil that glistened over his sparse dark hair.

"It's a pleasure, Miss Snow." The smooth tones of his polished accent washed over her. "And how are you enjoying Bar Harbor?"

"Very much. It's wonderful to be so close to the sea." She glanced at her mother to make sure she'd answered correctly, but there was nothing to fear. Marjorie was beaming.

"How marvelous. Indeed, in that lovely frock, you look like you just stepped out of the sea yourself. A veritable ocean goddess." The orchestra played the opening notes of a waltz, and he offered Lucy his hand. "May I have the honor of a dance?"

Lucy hesitated, and Marjorie shot her a warning look. She took a deep breath. "I would be delighted."

JAM POTS

"LUCY, YOU MIGHT COMPLAIN about the Duke of Crompton's hair oil, but I shall tell you right now, he is considered the smashing success of the summer. He is being taken up and he's been here a very short time." It was the day after the ball, and Lucy was walking with Marjorie to the Abenaki Club, where they'd been invited for tea.

Lucy was quickly learning the code in which her mother spoke. A corollary to "in the thick" was "to be taken up," which meant being ushered into the inner circles of the summer island society. The two words *inner circles*, however, brushed with the remnants of Marjorie's Southern accent, came out as "innuh suckles," which reminded Lucy of pigs at a trough.

Her mother stopped walking and turned to Lucy. She squinted at her for a moment. "Now, I would recommend not skinning your hair back quite so tightly under that bonnet but allowing a curl or two to show." She reached up under the brim of Lucy's hat and tugged at a tendril. "We don't want you looking too schoolmarmish."

"Oh, Mother, you know how I hate having my hair fussed with."

"Lucy, don't say that word '*hate*.' It's an ugly word and not becoming. '*Dislike*' perhaps, or '*not inclined*.'"

Lucy cocked her head a bit. "Do you really dislike Anna Green, Mother?"

"Now, why ever would you ask a thing like that? I don't dislike anybody. She is not our kind, that is all. It's not a question of dislike."

Lucy pressed her lips together as she readjusted her hat and began to walk on.

Marjorie quickened her pace to keep up with her. "I believe the duke enjoys art. You might tell him about that exhibit you went to last spring."

"The one about the Arctic at the natural history museum?"

"No no, not natural history. The painting exhibit at the armory. The one with the Stannish Whitman Wheeler paintings, particularly since Mr. Wheeler is to be in residence here this summer. It is an ideal topic of conversation."

With her curls now pulled down and bouncing in coquettish merriment, and armed with an ideal topic of conversation, Lucy supposed she was fit for the tea table. This time, they had been invited by Mrs. Van Wyck, Mrs. Forbes, and Mrs. Bannister, true bastions of the summer community.

"Why, do you know, he already has a jam pot with his name on it? Can you imagine? I think it is so quaint, this tradition of the club." Marjorie was talking nonstop as she expounded on the duke's virtues.

Lucy could not imagine how this "quaint tradition" could be so meaningful as to occupy so much of her mother's mind. The Abenaki jam pots were small wooden vessels that held a half cup of jam for the popovers that were served with afternoon tea. One had truly arrived in Bar Harbor society when one's name was painted on a jam pot. Apparently, the duke had reached this watershed moment in his social evolution on the island. Marjorie and the reverend had discussed thoroughly the possibility of their achieving this lofty pinnacle. The old bishop's pot, however, was still displayed on the shelf in the main parlor, and the Snows had agreed that because the bishop was still alive, it might seem awkward for there also to be a pot with their own surname inscribed.

Lucy and her mother crossed the lawn of the club and made their way up the wide stairway to the porch. The white fan-backed wicker chairs reminded Lucy of a gathering of gigantic butterflies.

"We don't want to be too early, or never too late. Ah! Perfect. Mrs. Bannister is here but not Mrs. Van Wyck or Mrs. Forbes. I think her daughter Matilda is coming. 'Muffy,' they call her, but perhaps you should call her Matilda. Doesn't pay to be too familiar right off the bat. You know she's engaged to the Earl of . . . of something or other."

"My dears, do sit down," Mrs. Bannister said, gesturing to the chairs. "The others will be here shortly, and I have taken the liberty of inviting the Duke of

Crompton. He is the most charming young man. We are all just mad for him. A very witty fellow. Life of any party. Ah, here he comes now with the Forbeses and Cornelia Van Wyck."

"Muffy just beat Tom Benedict soundly at tennis," the duke announced. "I can't imagine what she'll do to her future husband, the earl. They'll have to get those grass courts up to snuff when you arrive, my dear!"

"Grass!" Muffy said in a shocked voice. "I only play on clay. Well, Daddy will fix that."

"I'm sure he will." There was a slight mocking glint in his vivid dark eyes. Lucy looked over at her mother, who was rapt with attention and hanging on every word the duke said.

The duke continued, "I think that England can stand to learn a lot from young American ladies. We've become — how should I put it? — slightly stultified in our ways."

"How nice of you to say that, Your Grace." Lucy's mother was absolutely beaming.

"Firstly, no need to call me Your Grace, dear Mrs. Snow. Just Percy, if you please. And secondly, I didn't say it because it was nice. No, I mean it. We have much to learn from the likes of you." This time he looked directly at Lucy.

It was a gracious and handsome speech. With his refined manners, Percy was a welcome change from Eldon Drexel and the other young gentlemen she had met in New York. She must try to be pleasant to him, if only for her mother's sake. "I'm not sure if you saw it when you were in New York," Lucy began, "but there was a wonderful portrait exhibit of Stannish Whitman Wheeler." She gave a quick glance to her mother, who was nodding encouragingly. Then she absently lifted her hand and twirled a curl around her finger. *I can do this if I really try*, she thought. *It's not so bad.* She could feel the pleasure radiating from her mother like quiet ripples in a pond.

"Mr. Wheeler is to paint me," Matilda Forbes said eagerly. Lucy could tell she wasn't bragging but seemed truly excited by the opportunity.

"What an honor!" Lucy exclaimed. "Do you know what you might wear, Matilda?"

"Oh, you must call me Muffy," she said, smiling.

"And I have no idea what to wear. Perhaps you could help me choose?"

She heard her mother suppress a brief but ecstatic little yelp that was transformed into a quick cough.

"It would be my honor," Lucy said, feeling a flicker of pleasure. Muffy seemed so much nicer than Lenora Drexel or any of the young ladies she had met at the reception in New York.

"Oh, there you are, Dolly!" the duke exclaimed as the serving girl came up and set down two baskets of scones. "I wrote Mama in England about these scones. Do you suppose you could somehow coax the recipe from the cook?" He had been removing his gloves finger by finger, and Dolly seemed almost mesmerized by the graceful movements. She had already told the other girls in the kitchen about the elegant Englishman who wore fine gloves to tea in the heat of the afternoon. Lucy looked down and saw that his legs were crossed and he wore exquisite shoes of polished fawn-colored leather that looked almost as supple as that of his gloves. She thought wistfully of the dark, glowering sea boots of Phineas Heanssler, stained with salt water.

"Oh, it ain't difficult, sir," Dolly said, beaming. "I'll write it down for you myself. It's all in the baking, you know."

"No, I don't know, but I trust you do." Dolly nearly swooned. She was clearly charmed by the Duke of Crompton, who cut quite a figure with his lilac silk cravat and exquisitely tailored linen jacket with a bright wildflower in the lapel. He was as different from a Maine fisherman as one could imagine. Dolly set down the jam pots, all of which were inscribed except for the Snows', which seemed glaringly blank.

"I must say that I like the informality here, where we all know the staff by their first names, as opposed to Newport," the duke said as Dolly scurried out.

"Oh, Dolly Beal. Everyone knows the Beals," Mrs. Forbes replied. "She, her mother, her grandmother, and her great-grandmother have all worked here at the Abenaki. They are fixtures. Now, of course, in Newport when I was just a girl . . ."

As Mrs. Forbes and the duke compared notes on Newport and Bar Harbor, Lucy noticed her mother's eyes traveling from pot to pot. She could almost read her mind and commended her silently for keeping up the lively stream of conversation. Marjorie Snow did, however, manage to drop Aunt Prissy's name at least three times before the duke asked, "Is that Priscilla Bancroft Devries?"

"Indeed. We're from Baltimore. Prissy is Lucy's godmother. We have been best friends . . . well, really family, for years. As a matter of fact, Lucy has a dollhouse that Prissy gave her that is a replica of White Oaks."

"Really? How wonderful," the duke said.

"Yes. She simply adores Lucy."

"That does not surprise me." He smiled. "Does Mrs. Devries have children of her own?" the duke inquired.

"No, she was not blessed as we were." Marjorie reached over and gave Lucy's hand a squeeze. "Lucy is like a daughter to her. Her only child."

"I see," the duke said with a mild note of exclamation.

Lucy was uncomfortable with the direction the conversation was taking. She turned to Muffy and began asking her about her wedding to the Earl of Lyford.

"Charles Worth is making your dress? How exciting!"

"Yes, we're going to Paris in early September for fittings. Daddy wanted him to come here, but his schedule wouldn't permit. I am so happy! I really wish we could be married in Paris."

"Don't be ridiculous, darling!" her mother chimed in. "You'll be married in King's Chapel in Boston. That's how Forbeses do it."

Muffy made a delicate little moue with her mouth and rolled her eyes.

"The Reverend Snow performed the nuptials for Miss Phoebe Schuyler to John Drexel just this past spring," Marjorie interjected. "She also wore a Worth gown. It was . . . was simply magical! The man is a wizard, isn't he!"

This remark seemed to sit well with all at the table. The other women looked at her brightly, as if she had said something extremely clever and quite beyond the boundaries of the usual drabness of a minister's wife. Marjorie basked in the glow of their regard and wondered if a jam pot with their name might not be out of reach this summer.

STRANGELY WONDERFUL

IT HAD BEEN OVER A WEEK since Lucy had seen Phineas. She thought often of the fragrance of the boatyard, how the swirl of varnish, sawdust, and fresh paint mingled with the sea air. But his invitation, "come back anytime," had not been exercised. Was she to just walk right in carrying her tennis racket as before? Thankfully, there hadn't been many people around that day because it was a Saturday. She had been walking the same route she had before when they had encountered each other. Once, when she was in the post office mailing a letter for her father, she thrilled when she heard someone behind the counter yell into the backroom to ask if Phin Heanssler had picked up the package yet. She had almost been ready to offer her services as a courier. She thought of that now as she abruptly turned and headed toward the little red clapboard building.

"Ah, just the girl I've been looking for! This got left out of the batch we sent over to the rectory." Carrie Welles, the postmistress, held up a letter and waved it. "For you, I think. That is, if you are Lucy. Thinking of building a yacht?" She laughed. "Don't know why he decided to waste money on a stamp when he could have walked it over hisself. Guess those Heansslers make so much money from their yacht building that they can throw money about on stamps."

Lucy reached out for the letter. "Thank you," she murmured. She tried to appear calm, but her hand was trembling. Carrie Welles was a notorious snoop. The last time Lucy had come into the post office, she had seen the woman holding a letter up to the light as if to read the contents.

Lucy had a sinking feeling as she read the opening lines. So stiff, so formal, like he hardly knew her at all.

Dear Miss Snow,

A scarf was left on Desperate Lark. *We are not sure if it is yours or one of the other ladies' who was aboard that day, so I thought I would write you first to ask. I could either bring it by the rectory, or if it would not inconvenience you too much, you might stop by here to see if it is yours. Perhaps after church this Sunday?*

As Lucy read, her eyes opened with delight. The whole thing was an elaborate ruse. She had been wearing no scarf and he knew it. She felt a flutter in her chest as she tucked the letter into her pocket, safe from Carrie's prying eyes. He wanted to see her again.

After Sunday's early morning service, Lucy told her mother that she was not feeling well, and asked permission to go back to the house rather than attend the late morning service. There was always a reception afterward with iced tea and sandwiches, so there would be plenty of time for her to visit the boatyard before her parents returned home.

Phineas was waiting for her in the lofting room that overhung the first floor in the main part of the building. He leaned over the railing. "Come up here. I have something to show you."

"A scarf perhaps?" Lucy asked, raising one eyebrow.

He laughed. "Clever, wasn't it?"

"Very clever," she replied, and began walking up the stairs to the second floor.

She looked about her. Sunlight poured through the high windows of the lofting room. It was a simple, bright place where imagination and practicality met and were translated into a reality in the mysterious alchemy of the shipbuilder's mind, becoming yachts, fishing boats, coastal schooners, skiffs, and dories that could ply the seas in all sorts of weather.

Phineas was standing at a small drafting table. "Look at these." He indicated some photographs spread out on the table. "Here's a stool you can sit on." Lucy came over, climbed up on the swivel stool, and bent over them.

"That's me!"

"You at the helm, and you sitting there just when we first entered the channel, and some more of you at the helm."

"Gus gave these to you, Phineas?" Lucy asked. He nodded. It seemed odd to say they were good when they were all of her. So she looked at them one more time, then spun around on the stool to look about at the spacious loft.

It was an honest place with its scent of sawdust and salt air. On one wall hung a dozen or more wooden templates for drawing the sweeping elliptical lines of a hull. Beneath the templates was a bucket of colored chalk for making corrections on the blueprint that was spread out on the floor, and on one prominently placed shelf was the exquisitely crafted half model of the ship under construction. The master builder — in this case Phineas and not his father — had fashioned a hull form that was a scale model of the yacht to be built for the Van Wycks. The model was then cut down the center. One half was presented to the owner, the other kept by the shipbuilder. The varnished half model glistened in the sunlight, presiding over the lofting space like a sentry standing watch over the design. *Stay true to my lines, make me what I am intended to be.*

"So Gus made these prints just for you?"

"Yes, in his darkroom."

"He has his own darkroom?"

"There is very little the Bellamys do not have."

"That's what I don't understand. He gave you these, but you were not invited to the Bellamy party."

"We can't mix — native folk and summer folk. They never do."

"But you're not a servant. You're a yacht designer."

"Doesn't make any difference."

"But it does!" Lucy's eyes turned a stormy green.

He took a step forward and slowly raised his hand, cupping her chin with his slender but work-worn fingers. She shivered and he wrapped an arm around her. "It makes all the difference."

Before she could say another word, she felt both his arms wrapping around her. His mouth was on hers, pressing softly. He ran his fingers through her hair, and when their lips parted, she heard him whisper, "You make all the difference." She kept her eyes closed as they pulled away from each other. She kept her fingertips on his cheeks. There was a slight stubble. She ran her fingers over his skin and, finding his jawbone, traced it lightly. She felt them both enfolded by an intimacy she had never known or imagined, an irresistible intimacy that seemed rare and wonderful and that she wanted to explore more deeply. She turned her head slightly.

"I hope we're safe here?" She broke from his embrace to look around the lofting room, where the plans for a new yacht for the Van Wycks, even larger than the Bellamy yacht, had been drawn on the floor.

"We don't work on Sunday. Most people are in church. How did you escape?"

"I did not escape entirely. I went for the morning service but begged off the afternoon one." She smiled. "Headache, you know."

"Of course. Terrible, aren't they?" He grabbed her hand. "Let me show you to the master's cabin. All you need do is take off your shoes so you won't smudge the drawing."

A minute later, in bare feet they both walked across the plans toward the blue lines that were drawn to show where Sterling Van Wyck and his wife's bedroom would be built on the yacht.

"Funny how these rich people live, isn't it?" Lucy said as she sat on the floor of the Van Wyck bedroom.

"Is it really that funny to you?"

"Why, of course it is. Remember, I'm a reverend's daughter. Reverends don't have any money at all. We're only included, brought along because . . . well . . ." She was stumbling. "Because of God!" she blurted out. "People fear for their immortal souls as much as their bank accounts."

"And although they love the sea, they fear drowning in it."

"What do you mean?" Lucy asked.

"I must build sound ships to keep them safe on the high seas, and your father must minister to their souls to get them into heaven. We're all servants, in a sense living on the edges of their world to make sure they are safe."

She tipped her head to the side and smiled. So he didn't think of her as one of them, one of the tribe. That was both a relief and a joy. She turned and pointed to an area marked off with blue lines in one corner.

"What's this part?" Lucy said, pointing at the spot.

"Mr. Van Wyck's 'office.' Room for a desk and some books."

"And that door?" Lucy asked.

"Mrs. Van Wyck's boudoir."

"Her boudoir? On a yacht?"

"Yes, of course. She can't get undressed in front of her *husband*." He made an expression of mock horror. "Nor can he. That's how rich people do it. So on the port side, you'll see another door to his dressing room. So they don't have to see each other in their . . . well, altogether state." He suddenly broke out laughing. "My goodness, Lucy, your face is almost as red as your hair." He leaned forward and in the next second was pressing his mouth to hers.

The scent of sawdust swirled in the air. He pressed her harder and folded her in his arms. Then he pulled away and took her face in his hands as if he were holding something fragile. A shadow fled across the blue of his eyes.

"What is it?" she whispered.

"I'm afraid I'm never going to see you again."

"Don't say that!" Somehow she sensed that this had nothing to do with the rigid social order of this island world. It concerned a world that was only hinted at but neither really could grasp. Lucy felt shuddering dark fear sweep through her.

ETTIE'S SECRET

THERE WERE SECRETS and there were *secrets*, and this one almost hurt, Ettie thought as she crouched behind the trunk of a dark spruce tree that grew at the edge of the cove. It was a very high tide this evening, so the lavender rock from which Hannah always dove was completely awash. When Hannah dove, Ettie always felt this deep surge within herself, as if part of her own essence were rushing from her. And then with the first flash of the glittering tail that broke the water like a comet soaring from the very depths of the ocean, there came a crushing bitterness. Was it the secret that bothered her or, most likely, the envy and the fear that Hannah would leave one night forever?

There was another secret, of course, that was actually a lie. It was the secret of Lila, the oldest of the three Hawley daughters, who was in an asylum for the mentally ill in western Massachusetts. The lie was that she was said to be abroad studying art in a small village outside of Florence. It was not as if Ettie longed to blab this matter to the world at large. She only wanted to tell one person — Hannah Albury, who had been a servant in the Hawley household for almost two years.

Henrietta Hawley, or Ettie as she was called, at ten, almost eleven, was the youngest daughter of Horace and Edwina Hawley of Boston. Her best friend in the world was Hannah Albury. But the truth was that Ettie understood Hannah more than Hannah did her. Ettie knew Hannah's secret. But what Hannah did not comprehend was that just as Hannah longed to escape the land world, Ettie, despite her privilege, her Brahmin pedigree by virtue of belonging to one of Boston's oldest and most revered families, yearned to escape as well. Ettie found the world she was consigned to by her species and social rank stultifying, even smothering to the point of — yes — suffocation. And it would only get worse as she grew up.

Just that morning, she had been severely reprimanded by Miss Ardmore, her governess, for entering the drawing room barefoot. "No bare feet in the house!" Miss Ardmore had hissed.

"Why ever not?" Ettie had replied.

"It's unsanitary."

"Oh, hell's bells," Ettie blurted. Miss Ardmore had blanched.

"Ettie, you swore!"

"You call that swearing? I can do much worse than that. I know the word for the private parts of a bull and I can say —"

Miss Ardmore came up to her and clapped her hand over Ettie's mouth.

Yes, thought Ettie, "suffocating" was what it meant to grow up into a proper young lady.

And every day it was worse, and Ettie seemed to be gasping for more air. She felt like a fish out of water. Though she hesitated to use this expression, for Hannah was no mere fish; she was a sea creature.

Ettie was very disinclined to use the word *mermaid*. She detested the word *maid*. In her own mind, it meant either a servant or a rather witless young female. One of Ettie's major problems in life was how people thought about half the human race — unfortunately, the half she belonged to: female.

At this moment, she saw the flash of the tail. *Where does she go when she swims?* Ettie always wondered. She knew she could not follow Hannah there. She was not mer, but fully human. What did it mean, however, to be human? she sometimes wondered. In Ettie's world, it meant having half the fun, half the power. In Ettie's world, fun was defined rather narrowly in terms of a set of expectations. Her cousin Matilda "Muffy" Forbes had become engaged this summer. She was seventeen and what she expected and what had been expected of her could be written on a short list:

1. Make a proper marriage. The intended groom in this case was to be an earl from England with large estates. He needed Muffy's

money and she wanted a title. She would become a countess.

2. Muffy would have her "dozens," her dozens of dozens, the requisite twelve pairs of everything that were ordered for every bride.

3. Muffy would have children and they, too, would have titles — and if they were girls, Muffy would arrange their weddings and their dozens of dozens.

4. Muffy would over the years grow slightly fat, for the Forbeses had a tendency toward avoirdupois — a fabulous word for *fat* that she had learned from her governess.

5. Summers would be in Bar Harbor. Autumns in London for the season. Winter on the earl's estates in the countryside. Spring in Paris. Except now that there was money enough, Muffy was sure she could convince Morfit (*horrible name!* Ettie thought) to go to Paris for longer.

6. And then when she was a ripe old age, Muffy would simply keel over dead — hopefully, and not wind up like Big Adelaide, with her

locked eyes, being hauled around in a wheel-chair mute as a stone with her cranky old sister.

What difference did it make? They were all maids — old maids, young maids, even the married ones called matrons were still maids consigned to an eternally witless state. Ettie looked out to sea and again wondered where Hannah went. *Where does she swim to?*

⚜   ⚜   ⚜

As she swam out toward the cave to meet May, Hannah wondered if her life could get any more complicated. Stannish Whitman Wheeler's angry words still echoed in her ears.

"You're going to have to decide, Hannah. Soon. You can't have it both ways. I can make a life for you here on land."

"But I might die on land."

"You won't. You'll adapt. We'll be married."

"Stannish Whitman Wheeler marry a servant girl? You'll lose all your clients and I'll lose the sea."

They had been arguing like this for months and it had gotten them nowhere. But ever since the discovery that her and May's third sister had arrived, she had become more outspoken with Stannish. Should she give up the family that was almost complete for marriage? Stannish had given up the sea for his painting, but was she willing to give it up for him? The worst was when Stannish would almost cavalierly say to her, "You'll get used to it. You'll see. At first you might miss it a bit, but then it's just like an old scratch. It heals over very fast. A scar you won't feel at all."

That was just the problem; she felt everything because she was mer. It made the world around her more vibrant — and even harder to leave behind.

⚜ ⚜ ⚜

"Look!" May said as Hannah swam into the cave. She was holding a piece of paper.

"What is it?" Hannah asked.

"Come up close and see. Don't get it wet, though. It's a watercolor."

"What a lovely drawing," Hannah whispered. "She

wants to meet us. Can't you see? It's clear as any-thing, May." Her voice cracked and she began to cry.

"Hannah, whatever is the matter?" May put her arm around her sister's shoulders.

"He was one of us," Hannah said, with tears trick-ling down her cheeks.

May felt a dread begin to stir deep inside her. She twitched the flukes of her tail, still suspended in the water, and tightened her grip around Hannah. "Who? Who are you talking about?"

"Stannish Whitman Wheeler." Hannah spoke his name in a barely audible voice.

"The painter?"

Hannah nodded.

A coldness crept through May. She shivered and the scales on her tail scintillated darkly as fear radi-ated through her entire being. She sensed what Hannah was going to say next. It was something she had never mentioned to Hannah, had almost been afraid to mention.

"He mistook you for me one day in the village, didn't he?" Hannah asked.

"Yes," May said. Her voice was barely audible.

"In that alley, he saw only the back of your head, your hair, and thought you were me. You see, May, he is . . . is . . . ," she whispered. "My sweetheart."

"But you say he is mer."

"*Was* mer. He can't go back."

"Why not?"

"It's the Laws of Salt, May. If he tried to return to the sea, he would drown." May gasped. "We love each other so much. Can you think of anything worse?"

May bit her lip lightly. "Maybe." She thought of Hugh Fitzsimmons, those lovely gray eyes that endlessly intrigued and charmed her. His funny, slightly crooked smile and how those eyes would sparkle when he laughed.

"I, too, have a sweetheart, but he was never mer. He never had a choice."

ENTAILMENTS

IT WAS LATE IN THE EVENING, and Lucy had just come from her bedroom to fetch a book she had been reading and forgotten to take with her. Both her parents were in the small parlor. Her father was reading, her mother sewing somewhat resentfully as she repaired a small tear in the reverend's vestments.

"Lucy, when you met the duke at the Quoddy Club this morning, you really shouldn't have — have —" She began to stammer.

"Have? Have what? Mother, I was perfectly friendly."

"You were friendly but so mercilessly intellectual and then when you mentioned Oscar Wilde — that man is scandalous."

"Mother, he is a playwright, a famous one, and the duke knows him, along with James Whistler." She did not mention that he also knew Lily Langtry, a truly shameless beauty who was rumored to be having an affair with the Prince of Wales. The duke kept very exciting company in England. He went to every art opening and every play.

She flashed back to his eloquent description of the Elgin Marbles. "If you stand before them, Lucy, you cannot quite believe they are made of stone. It is as if you are transgressing some border where time and matter melt and you become part . . . part . . ." He had paused as if to search for a word.

"Part of a dream."

"Exactly. An ancient dream that is on the continuum of eternity."

"I just don't understand, Mother. I was genuinely interested in what he was saying about his life in London and the museums, and I thought I was being friendly enough."

"My dear." Her father looked up from his reading. "Friendliness is not something that should be doled out in measured quantities like a cup of sugar."

Lucy grew still and waited several seconds before answering. She dared not tell her parents about Phineas, for whom she had unlimited quantities of "friendliness." She looked up at her mother and smiled. "I'll try to be less intellectual, Mother, and more *friendly*."

Marjorie Snow's face relaxed. She picked up Lucy's hand, pressed it to her midriff, and gave it a squeeze. "This is a chance. He is truly interested in you. He's a duke. You could be a duchess. That, I think, outranks an earl. Like Muffy Forbes's Earl of Lyford. She'd only be an earless, I think."

"No, dear," said the reverend, who at the moment had been reading a book entitled *Rank and Nobility: The Guide to Peerage of the British Empire*. "Muffy Forbes will be a countess. The Countess of Lyford. I find her quite charming. She has offered to join the altar guild and direct the arranging of flowers for Sunday services. She suggests native plants — lupine and the like, which is in season now, along with daisies. I told her that you would be happy to join the guild, too, Lucy. I think it would provide an invaluable contact for you."

"Oh, yes, Lucy, invaluable," her mother echoed. "Now don't be stubborn."

Joining the altar guild was easy, Lucy thought. It was a way to offer a modicum of instant gratification to her parents. "Oh, yes, Father, I would be happy to join the altar guild. Muffy seems lovely."

"She is, and a very good catch for the earl," her mother replied.

"But, Mother, don't you see? Muffy is very wealthy." She did not want to quote Gus Bellamy verbatim, but she also did not want her parents to be misled in any way. They surely could not be so benighted as to not be aware of the value of a substantial dowry.

Their contrivances to move into "the thick" had seemed innocent enough at first. Of course it would be lovely if her father could become the bishop of New York. But she realized clearly now that he was not the only candidate for higher office. Their designs extended to her. And in the brief days since the Bellamy party, her mother had plunged into a vigorous pursuit of the Duke of Crompton. She had contrived another meeting at the Abenaki for tea and had also managed for Lucy and herself to have an "accidental" encounter with the duke in the card room at the Quoddy Club.

"You know we aren't rich like the Forbeses."

"That shouldn't make any difference," her mother said firmly. "You are much prettier than Muffy."

"Mother, these titled young men are not looking for beauty. They are looking for money."

"Not necessarily, my dear," her father said. "They are impressed with background, culture, position. I don't want to spill any beans here, but there is buzz about the office of the bishop. Vanderwaker's resignation is expected by the end of the month."

"And," Marjorie Snow chimed in, "the young duke was quite impressed with our connections with the Bancrofts."

"Aunt Prissy?"

"Yes, Aunt Prissy. He knows all about her family and you see, dear, unlike the Bancrofts with those onerous entailments, the duke's family has none, no entailments."

"Entailments?" Lucy asked.

"Yes, entailments. That's what they call it when property or a fortune can only be inherited by a male."

"But I am not a male."

"Of course not."

"Nor was Aunt Prissy."

Marjorie Snow turned to her husband in frustration. "Oh, Stephen, explain all this to Lucy. It's too complicated for me," she said, petulantly jabbing the needle through the cloth.

Stephen Snow, upon rising from his chair, bumped the side table. There was a small thud as a Bible slipped off. Lucy quickly picked it up and restored it to its place with the other reading matter. Her father was still holding the book of peerage as he spoke.

"It is not all that complex. In England, entailed property is usually inherited by the eldest male in the family."

"But Aunt Prissy isn't English."

"Lucy, don't interrupt when I am speaking," the reverend said, rather sharply.

"Sorry, Father."

"Now may I continue?" Lucy was irritated by this disingenuous request. A spark of rebellion flared within her. *What if I said no?* The very thought caught her off guard. This defiance, these mutinous notions, where did they come from? She took a deep breath to dispel her anger. "You see, Lucy," her father continued, "Percy Wilgrew, the Duke of Crompton, has no older brothers. Nor any male cousins. The coast is clear, so to speak. Do you understand?"

"Yes, Father," she replied with appropriate docility, a docility she did not feel in the least. There was so much more she wanted to say.

"You are a special girl, Lucy. I think the duke sees that."

"He does?"

"He came to afternoon services last Sunday. He was surprised you weren't there, but we told him that you had a headache, and do you know what he said?"

"What?" Lucy's heart raced. This was exactly the time she had been "suffering her headache" in the arms of Phineas.

"He said it was probably from all that reading you do. That he had never met such a well-read young lady."

"Look, she's blushing, Stephen. See, every girl loves a compliment."

Lucy was indeed blushing. Her parents looked so happy. She wanted so to please them. She thought of the adoption papers she had discovered in her father's desk years before, the haunting words *mother unknown*. And here was a mother known, right before her. A mother and a father who had sought her out, chosen her. She imagined babies lined up in little crates like fresh produce in the market. She pictured her parents walking along and examining each one, picking it up as one might pick up an apple to see if there were any bruises, and in fact she did have a "bruise," her turned foot. But nevertheless they had chosen her. They wanted her and they wanted the best for her. They considered the duke the best and perhaps he was. She had been captivated by his description of the Elgin Marbles and his estate with a lovely winding river that passed not a quarter of a mile from his home.

"Oh, and, Lucy darling, would you do me the greatest favor?"

"Of course, Mother. What is it?"

"I have a note for you to deliver to Mrs. Van Wyck thanking her for those extraordinary lilies she sent for the altar. Might you deliver this to her?" She held out a small cream-colored envelope.

"I would be happy to, Mother."

"That's a good girl."

TWO PATHS

SHE HAD JUST ROUNDED the bend when she heard someone call her name. It was Phineas.

Lucy felt her stomach twist. The memory of their kiss sent shivers down her spine, but she had just promised her parents she would try harder with the duke.

She could not even imagine the horror she would face if they knew of her attraction to a "native." Indeed she might as well go off to the Arctic and marry an Inuit.

"Wh-what are you doing here?" she stammered.

"Come to see Mr. Van Wyck about his yacht." Under his arm he carried a tubular canvas satchel. "Some changes in the drawings."

"I see," she said, fingering the fringe on her shawl and trying to avoid looking at him. "Well, you'll have to excuse me. I'm in a bit of a rush."

"What brought you here?"

"Oh, nothing that would interest you." She winced as the words slipped from her mouth.

"Lucy, are you all right?"

His concern made her heart twinge, and it was all she could do not to throw her arms around him. But then she imagined the look of dismay on her parents' faces.

"I'm perfectly well, thank you."

He took a step forward. "Lucy —"

She moved to the side to avoid his outstretched arm. "Good day, Mr. Heanssler."

"You just seem a little … Never mind!" he said sharply. Then he nodded toward a sign that she had not previously noticed, which read SERVICE ENTRANCE. "I'll be going this way," he said pointedly.

"Yes, I suppose so." She dared not look him in the eyes but continued on the main path, the proper path for a possible duchess, to Wyckmore, the Van Wyck cottage.

"Oh, thank you, my dear! How kind of your mother to send you. Please sit down for a moment and chat. Can I offer you something to drink — tea? — lemonade? It's already so hot."

Lucy stared at Mrs. Van Wyck in a sort of daze as the conversation with Phineas buzzed in her head.

"Lucy?"

"Oh, that's very kind, but I'm afraid I can't stay. I am actually in a bit of a hurry. I have . . . I have" — she searched for an excuse — "to meet someone."

"Not the Duke of Crompton?" Mrs. Van Wyck said this with a coquettish tilt to her head, and her small dark eyes sparkled conspiratorially as if to invite a confidence.

"Oh, no . . . no."

"But he's quite nice, don't you agree?"

"Oh, yes, lovely." Was she becoming a project for Mrs. Van Wyck as well as for Gus's mother? How could all these people have such an interest in her?

"You know he is quite a good friend of the Prince of Wales."

"No, I didn't know that." She was about to wonder what Lenora Drexel or Elsie Ogmont would think if they knew she was socializing with a member of the prince's inner circle, but then Phineas's face erased all other images. How could she have spoken to him in that tone?

"Yes, he's very well connected." Mrs. Van Wyck sighed. "He is truly a man of the world. You know, American husbands tend to be such sticks-in-the-mud. I mean, my dear husband, Sterling, is wonderful, but I really have to nearly pry him away from his office to get him to go anywhere. Percy has such a joie de vivre. He's always ready for fun. And a real sense of style. So fashionable." Lucy couldn't help but think that the reason Sterling had to be pried loose was owing to the fact that he was making a living, whereas these English lords did not have any jobs to speak of. "So well connected," she said again. "You know he has a seat in parliament, the House of Lords, of course. His grandfather was the chancellor of the exchequer, and often that office leads to prime minister, and there's talk of the duke making a fine chancellor as well. Can you believe it?"

Lucy was unsure of what Mrs. Van Wyck was asking her to believe. So she just murmured, "Oh, my." That seemed to be the safest response. "I had better be on my way, but thank you again. And Mother said she just loved the lilies."

"I thought she would, coming from Baltimore. They are such a Southern flower. I know that her cousin Priscilla Bancroft has raised some prize ones."

Mother's cousin! Lucy tried to disguise her dismay.

"In fact I think there is one named for her by a breeder. The Priscilla or something like that."

"Yes, I believe there is." *Good Lord,* Lucy thought, *the next thing there will be rumors of one named the Marjorie!*

Lucy could not get away from the house fast enough. She felt a fury rising inside her. She was becoming a "project" for a bunch of bored, too-rich women who had nothing better to do.

Lucy's eyes began to dart about Mrs. Van Wyck's sun porch. How could her mother have lied like this? Did her father know? They loved her, she knew that, but this was too much. This room in which she sat with Mrs. Van Wyck suddenly seemed small and air-less. She did not complete the thought. She made her excuses to leave and nearly ran out the front door.

The path ahead of her blurred, for her eyes had filled with tears as she ran. When she reached the place where she and Phin had parted, a sob tore from her as she spied the sign SERVICE ENTRANCE. It loomed in the shadows of the tall spruce trees like a harsh recrimination. Why had she treated him so horribly? Had she really lost her only chance at hap-piness all because she was trying to please her parents, her mother, who had spun this fantasy about Prissy Bancroft? This was a world with signposts to tell one which path to follow. But was there any for someone like herself? Was there a third path, a way where one did not have to lie about anything? Where you could be who you really are?

It was dusk by the time she approached her par-ents' cottage, and she could hear the tide already lapping high on the cliff rocks. She knew she was too agitated to go into the parlor where they would be sitting, her mother with her needlepoint, her father reading his church correspondence from New York, or perhaps the Bulletin of the Dioceses. She simply could not face them. She sat by the cliff for a long time, until the moon began to rise. The liquid splash of the sea against the granite was a soothing song, so she turned toward the cliff path.

The tide had completely obliterated the beach and laid down a silver track to the rocks at the cliff's base. She pulled off her dress and stood in her chemise and then petticoat. Her way to the cave was blocked. She imagined that the sloping rock she usually sat on in the cave would be completely submerged. She drew back. *What am I afraid of?* The soft wind blew her petticoat around her calves as if to tease her. She sat down on the very brink of the ledge. The water slipped over her knees to her thighs. She bent over. There was a sudden radiance issuing from beneath her hem that took her breath away. *It's easy,* she thought, and slipped in. For a brief moment, she was upright in the water. The skirt of her slip swirled about her like the petals of a flower. *Let go! Let go!* a voice in her head whispered. She slid under the water and felt the curl and pull of the tide. *I am swimming!* The water deepened. She dove. She was now sliding through a tapestry of undulating amber sea grapes that, while dry and pallid onshore, now made her feel as if she were passing through spangles of tawny gold. She was unsure how long she had been swimming, but she realized abruptly that she had not taken a breath. She paused to consider this and rolled over onto her back still beneath the surface. The dark water sparkled with iridescent colors as if a watery rainbow had come aborning from the depths of the sea. It took her a moment to realize that it was not a rainbow. Her feet and legs had disappeared, replaced by a tail. The scales ranged from hues of emerald green to aquamarine and the softest pinks. *I have no feet. I have no knees nor thighs. I have a tail! I am not their kind or "our" kind, I am my kind! A daughter of the sea.* And somewhere she was sure she had a family.

She dove straight to the bottom to the seafloor, then, with a power she never even dreamed she possessed, she shot up, breaking through the surface, and leaped for the sliver of the moon.

17

BAR HARBOR RULES

THE SWEEPING LAWN of the Hawley estate, Gladrock, allowed for three separate croquet fields to be set up. Not all the guests played, of course. There were small round tea tables scattered about, covered with creamy white linens, and servants circulating with platters of sandwiches, iced tea, and lemonade as well as salad plates with generous scoops of crabmeat nestled in ruffles of lettuce. It was well known that the Hawleys' Mrs. Bletchley was the best cook on the island. When platters were brought forth with profiteroles, meringues, and tiny tarts, they always created a sensation with people who compared the delicate confections to jewelry, for they were exquisitely decorated with glazed berries, silver sugar dragées, confectioner's confetti, and colored sugar crystals.

Those who were not eating or playing croquet wandered through the winding paths of the rose maze, or they could visit the greenhouses where Edwina Hawley raised her prizewinning orchids, or perhaps proceeded to her most recently established horticultural folly — a topiary garden.

But at the moment, all three croquet fields were in use, with ladies and gentlemen and a few youngsters chasing colored balls around with mallets.

Lucy found herself in a group of six that included Percy Wilgrew, two middle-aged gentlemen who were brothers, a young Hawley girl of about ten, and a woman who was apparently her governess.

Although the duke was not Lucy's partner — she'd been paired with one of the middle-aged gentlemen, Godfrey Appleton — it seemed that he thought otherwise. Indeed, the duke completely ignored his own partner, the governess, Miss Ardmore, as Lucy was lining up her next shot.

"I believe if you take the wicket from about a

twenty-degree angle off to the left, you'll get through free and clear." He paused. "But, oh, dear, I might be making this unnecessarily complicated for you. Do you understand degrees?"

Ettie Hawley gasped and Lucy looked up, her green eyes barely concealing her temper.

"Uncle God, how insulting is that!" Ettie hissed. "Besides, he should be helping Miss Ardmore and not the competition."

Godfrey Appleton gave his niece's shoulder a pat. "Calm yourself," he whispered. "I think Miss Snow can take care of herself."

"Your Grace," Lucy began, for that was how her father said one was to address a duke.

"Oh, please, not such formality. We are not in court but on a croquet field in this beautiful place, Gladrock." He swept his hand in an almost proprietary gesture.

"Precisely, and though it might surprise you or perhaps alarm you, I know exactly what a twenty-degree angle is even though I am not carrying a protractor." With that she stepped forward and gave the ball a firm tap that sent it straight through the wicket, which gave her a bonus shot.

Ettie looked up at her uncle Godfrey and gave him a nudge with her elbow.

"Smashing performance!" the duke exclaimed.

Ettie nudged her uncle again and gave him a devilish look. "Watch me, Uncle God. I'm going to wrap this up."

Ettie's yellow ball was ahead and on her bonus shot, she hit the duke's ball on her way through the wicket.

"Yay!" she whooped most indecorously. "Two bonus shots for me."

"Two shots for hitting me, Miss Hawley?" the duke asked.

"Yes, Bar Harbor rules." She looked at him grimly. "And wait till you see this."

Ettie was lined up for the last wicket on the field.

Her uncle Godfrey had sidled up to his brother. "Yes, just wait. The little savage has been unleashed."

Ettie slammed the croquet ball through the last wicket, hitting the post.

Miss Ardmore shuddered as her charge let out another wild whoop. "Poison! I'm poison," Ettie screamed.

"Let the rampage begin!" Barkley said.

Ettie came back through the wicket, gaining herself another two bonus points (Bar Harbor rules). For her first bonus point, she came within three or four yards of the duke's ball.

"Oh, my!" He grasped his chest. "Cruel maid, she is after me!"

"I'm not a maid!" Ettie muttered between clenched teeth. She hit her ball through the nearest wicket, which earned her another bonus point. She picked up the ball and brought it next to the duke's, then put her foot on it, getting set for what was called a roquette hit.

"Wait a minute! You're not roquetting me?" the duke protested.

"Indeed I am," Ettie answered coolly.

"Are these Bar Harbor rules again?"

"No, Gladrock rules." And she whacked the duke's ball to kingdom come. "Death blow!" Ettie raised her mallet in the air and, stomping the grass, launched into a fierce little dance.

"I think she's a most peculiar child," the duke leaned over and whispered to Lucy.

Lucy was laughing and took off her hat to fan herself. "I think she is wonderful!"

Ettie had been glorying in her triumph just as Lucy took off her hat and some pale red ringlets fell down from the upswept knot her mother had arranged. Ettie blinked. *She looks so much like Hannah.* Her hair was paler and her nose a bit sharper. But her eyes were the same intense green. Ettie supposed she hadn't noticed before because Lucy had been wearing her hat, and her face was in the shadows.

At the same moment, someone else noticed the young lady fanning herself with her brimmed hat. The clatter of a pitcher was heard falling on the dessert table.

"Oh, dear, I am so sorry!" Hannah said as she scurried to clean up the mess.

"Don't worry," Florrie, the other maid, said.

"Mrs. Bletchley will have my head. Look, I've spoiled the meringues."

"Only a couple," Florrie replied. "Run into the kitchen and fetch some more, and some cloths to mop this up. Look, nothing is broken."

"I'm not sure what happened," Hannah said.

"Well, you look rather flushed. Maybe the heat got to you."

"Yes, maybe."

"Go in and get a nice cool drink and rinse off your face. That'll help."

Hannah rushed back inside. She stopped in the breezeway outside the kitchen to catch her breath. It was just such a shock. She hadn't been expecting it. But when the girl took off her hat, she knew in an instant that she was the one. And she also knew that she, her sister, had crossed over at last.

⚜ ⚜ ⚜

On another island, known as Barra Head, far across the sea, the southernmost island of the chain known as the Hebrides, a woman perched on a granite slab in a cave. She had been tuning a small

Scottish harp, a *clàrsach* — no easy task. The first two strings were set to the same pitch. But on this morning, as Avalonia set to turning the pegs of the strings with her tuning key, she knew as soon as she plucked them that they were perfect. She felt a deep vibration within herself, an unearthly harmony as if there were strings inside her own body. She could hardly tell where she ended and the harp began. It was as if they had become one continuous living form. She knew instantly the meaning of the deep yet surging resonance that seemed to build within her. The third of her sister Laurentia's children lived and would soon find the other two. The Laws of Salt were roiling through her veins. And if she were patient, the three young girls might find her as well. She leaned the small harp against her shoulder and began to sing

Bye loo bye loo
Mer child of the sea
Bye loo bye loo
Twixt water and land we be
On land we are both maid and man
Bye loo bye loo

CHORDS FROM ACROSS THE SEA

THE HAWLEY HOUSE was quiet. Every servant was out on the lawn watching the fireworks. Hannah had pled illness, and Mrs. Bletchley had sent her to bed, telling her not to worry about the ruined meringues. However, Hannah was anything but ill. She had to get to the water. She knew she could not go out the back way, for everyone was on the lawn looking at the fireworks. She thought it would be better to leave through the French doors by the conservatory and then run directly into the small birch grove. From there she could follow a path to the sea. She had planned to go out later to meet with Stannish, but he would have to wait. Her sister had crossed over.

As she was passing through the conservatory,

Hannah caught a glimpse of the harp. It had intrigued her ever since she had come to work for the Hawleys. With its curved golden wood that seemed like a disembodied wing, it had become a kind of musical incarnation of an angel. It was in the music room of the Hawleys' Boston house on Beacon Hill that she had first met Stannish, when he had come to paint portraits of the Hawley daughters.

Hannah could play the harp, although she had never had lessons. It was similar to how she discovered she could swim. There had been a ferocious storm in Boston, and the roar of the thunder shaking the roof had created a separate vibration that resonated deeply within Hannah as she slept. She had crept downstairs and discovered that those vibrations were emanating from the harp. Almost in a trance, she walked toward the harp and sat down. Like swimming, it was an instinct. She began to play. The cacophony of the storm camouflaged the music for the rest of the sleeping household.

Tonight on her way through the conservatory, the harp beckoned her again. There was no storm. Could the strings be vibrating to the sound of the fire-works? *I can't stop now*, she thought. She had to get to the water. But she closed her eyes for a moment and set her hand lightly upon the sound box of the harp, and then slid her hand up to the harmonic arch. No, she thought. These strings were rousing to the vibrations of another harp, other strings from far, far away. A chord had been struck and with it she could almost hear a voice.

Hannah slipped into the water on Seal Point, a cove at the back of Gladrock. It was farther from the spot in the cove where she usually entered, but over one hundred people were now gathered on that shore to watch the fireworks. She had to swim to Egg Rock fast and fetch May.

As she rounded the point, two seals, old companions of hers, slid from the ledges to accompany her. They seemed to sense her urgency this evening and swam quietly by her side, making no attempt to distract her with their usual playful antics.

She dove deep as she swam into the sweeping flare of the Egg Rock Lighthouse. She didn't want May's father to see her. She would climb out of the water and then creep under May's window and flick pebbles against the pane. Normally, they left messages for each other in the cave, but Lucy had crossed over sooner than either one of them had expected. Hannah felt desperate to get to Egg Rock. The distance was long enough as it was and now the tide had changed and was against her, slowing her down even more. But she had only one thought — she and May would soon meet their sister.

High in the lantern room of the lighthouse, May Plum was filling the lamp that flashed the signature signal — two bright bursts of light followed by a ten-second gap.

It was a clear evening, and May wished that Hannah did not have to work, for she could think of nothing lovelier than swimming out to sea to watch the fireworks. The moon was still just a sliver, so the sky jeweled with the embers of the fireworks would be so beautiful. She walked onto the rail that encircled the top of the lighthouse and leaned out into the night in the direction of the booms of the firecrackers. She could swim out alone, she supposed, but it wouldn't be as much fun. The locket she always wore swung out a bit and she became aware of a peculiar feeling. A kindling from within.

Inside that locket were a few of the tiny teardrop crystals from the sea chest tucked away in the secret closet. The crystals had been embedded in the blanket in which she had been swaddled as an infant. This sensation of warmth and light had happened only once before. It was right before May had crossed over.

She touched the locket. It was warm. "*She's crossed,*" May whispered to herself. *She's crossed and Hannah knows and she's out there. Coming for me.* May tore down the stairs of the lighthouse.

Gar Plum heard her go. But he knew he could do nothing. Every time he heard May leave in the middle of the night, he could only hope she would return.

It was inevitable, he thought. Even that young beau from Harvard might not keep her on land. But if this was God's plan for May . . . well, what right did he have interfering? There was one thing Edgar Plum was sure of — strange as his beloved daughter might be, she was one of God's creatures.

GOD'S CREATURES

THE HAWLEYS' Fourth of July celebration extended well into the evening, for the croquet match was followed by tea dancing, then a garden supper, and when darkness fell, the fireworks began. Percy Wilgrew stuck to Lucy like flypaper. She could feel the other young ladies glaring at her from the arms of their considerably less distinguished escorts, but at that moment, Lucy would've gladly let them have him. All she could think about was Phineas. His words from the time they had first kissed came back to her. "I'm afraid I'm never going to see you again," a prophecy that she had caused to come true.

She felt there was no one at the party she could truly talk to, and there seemed to be no potted palms to hide behind. She had looked around for Gus after the croquet game, but he seemed to have vanished. Most likely he had planned a rendezvous with Anna Green. It was a bittersweet thought, for though she was pleased for Gus, she envied him.

Lucy had finally attached herself to Muffy Forbes and Muffy's young brother, Arthur, who was about thirteen and was a fun, lively sort. But then her mother had come over to drag her off to meet some Van Wyck or other. Finally, feigning illness, Lucy found her father.

"But the fireworks, my dear?"

"No, Father, I really can't stay. I'm . . . I'm afraid I might be sick." At first she thought she was lying, but a wave of nausea swept over her.

"I'll get you home, dear. Let's not disturb your mother."

In the drive of the Hawley estate was a line of small carriages that had conveyed many of the guests to the festivities.

Petey Beal, who had helped the Snows move into the cottage, was sitting on the seat of the first one.

"Hello, Petey. Lucy is feeling a bit faint. Could you give us a lift back to the cottage?"

"You bet, Reverend Snow."

Just then, there was the boom and crackle of the first of the fireworks. A tracery of blue embers embroidered the night.

"Father, you stay. It will be so beautiful. I'll be fine once I get home."

"I'll take care of her, Reverend, don't you worry."

"Are you sure, Lucy? You don't want me to come?"

"I'll be fine."

Lucy sank back into the seat as Petey tapped the horse with the whip, and the wheels creaked.

As they pulled away from the party, Lucy felt the nausea begin to recede. She was heading toward home — her real home. The drive took only ten minutes.

"You sure you don't want me to take you down the path, Miss Snow?" Petey asked.

"I'm sure, Petey. I feel better already. Please go along. I'm sure you want to see the fireworks. I can still hear them."

"You'll have a good view from here as well I think, miss."

"Thank you so much."

"Pleasure, miss."

Lucy did not even go back into the cottage. She had to return to the water. She climbed down the cliff, tore off the dress and, in her petticoats, waded into the sea.

When she had first plunged into the water, she had not headed toward the cave but straight out to sea because she felt the need to get as far away as possible from everything to do with land. The Duke of Hair Oil, as she now thought of him. Her mother, who had obviously embellished beyond reason their connection with Aunt Prissy, and her father and what were now his ceaseless discourses on rank, nobility, and titles of the English aristocracy. It all revolted her. She was so disgusted and so angry she did not realize how far she had swum from land.

But now she made her way back to the cave and, swimming into it, hoped against hope she would find them there. A million questions streamed through her mind. Who were they? Surely if she had seen them in the village or at one of the parties, she might have sensed who they were. But perhaps they lived all the time in the sea. Was this possible?

The cave was unusually dark as she swam in. The new moon was already too high to light it, but she suddenly saw an incandescent flickering at the end. She blinked. Two girls sat on the ledge, their radiant tails half in the water. One girl's tail was a deep rose and amber with waves of green. The other's tail was shades of violet and gold. The three of them looked at one another for several seconds as if what they saw was not quite real but a vision. Finally, one spoke in a hushed voice.

"We've been waiting!" she said.

Lucy looked from one girl's face to the other. It was as if she were looking in a mirror and seeing an image so very similar yet not really identical. She swam up to them slowly. "Who are you?" she asked.

"Your sisters," the girl with the amber tail answered.

The other girl reached out her hand. Lucy touched it tentatively, as if expecting her to vanish.

"My sisters?" She thought of that seminal image — the apples in a crate at a market. *They picked me but not these two?* They must have been together at some time, but for how long? Why was it only now after all these years they were meeting? And what destiny had brought them together now?

And yet, even in the swirl of questions, one thought burst forward. How could these dazzling creatures be her sisters? They seemed so free. Free of all the things of land that plagued her, all the artifices, the duplicities, the ridiculous encrustations of "tribal life." "I — I," she stammered. "I don't even know your names."

"I'm May," said the one with the violet-hued tail.

"And I'm Hannah. I saw you today at the Hawleys'."

The weight of this statement almost knocked Lucy's breath from her.

"You did. But I didn't see you." She couldn't believe she'd walked by her own sister only hours earlier.

"I'm a servant." Hannah smiled wryly. "We tend to be invisible. But the moment I saw you, I knew who you were and that you had crossed over at last."

"Is that what you call it?" Both girls nodded. "But where do we come from? How did this happen?"

May inhaled deeply. "It's a long story, and we don't know all the answers."

The two girls took turns telling her how they'd discovered they were mer. Lucy was transfixed. For the first time, she realized that deep down inside she had always felt a sense of desolation, otherness, that went beyond her inability to make small talk at parties. But now that sensation began to ebb just as the tide.

They were sisters, but they differed in slight ways. Hannah definitely had the reddest hair, and Lucy herself had the palest. May's eyes were green but with flecks of gold and what seemed almost turquoise. Hannah's face was more rounded, May's a bit sharper. May had the thick downeast accent of the island people, but Hannah spoke with no trace of any accent. Lucy learned that Hannah came only in the summer, for she was a servant for the Hawleys in Boston in the winter. She had started out as a scullery girl but rose quickly through the ranks and had even accompanied the family on their annual sojourn to Paris.

May's life by contrast seemed endlessly dreary to Lucy. She lived on Egg Rock. She was the daughter of the lighthouse keeper and his invalid wife, who was something of a terror.

She told Lucy how she had first spied her when the steamer the *Elizabeth M. Prouty* had entered the passage between Egg Rock and Bar Harbor.

"That's how she spotted me, too!" Hannah said. "And she had to wait all last summer for me to cross."

"So you were the first, May?"

"Yes. I was the first."

"How did you figure it out?" Something in May's face made Lucy wonder if her sister's transformation had been a bit more trying than her own.

"I was drawn like you and Hannah were, but my father would never let me even dip a toe into the water. You see, he was the one who found me."

"How?"

"Drifting in a sea chest." May closed her eyes for a moment as if she were trying to reach back in time to those first days in her life, to the sensation of the waves and the moment Gar had plucked her from the chest and wrapped her in his foul-weather gear.

"A sea chest?"

"From a shipwreck. The wreck of the HMS *Resolute*."

And then May began to tell her about the secret little closet where she had discovered the chest and the letters exchanged between Gar Plum and the Revenue Cutter Service.

Then May and Hannah told her about the big swim they'd made the previous summer to the wreck of the HMS *Resolute* off the Nantucket Shoals.

Lucy did not speak for almost an entire minute when they had finished their story. Finally, she said, "You say that the figurehead is that of our mother?"

Her sisters both nodded gravely.

"Her face is just like ours," Hannah said. "I mean I know we all look a bit different. But there is no denying the face of this woman."

"She's our mum," May said.

Hannah pressed her lips together firmly and shook her head slightly up and down. "No doubt about it!"

Mum, thought Lucy. She savored its sound. It was such an intimate word, possessing a cozy resonance. She had never called her mother Mum, just Mother. She wondered for the first time if she had even as a baby called her Mama.

"Mum." She repeated the word softly, as if she were tasting it. She had to press her lips together twice to say it. "Mum," she repeated for a third time. A smile lit her face. "When can we go? How long does it take?"

"We can do it in a night of hard swimming," Hannah said. "May knows all about currents."

"Yes, there is one off Grand Manan. It's very powerful. We can catch it on the way south and west, and then catch the counter one coming back. They flow strong this time of year."

"I want to go. I want to go now. You say the figurehead looks like us? You can tell she really was our mother, our true mother?" She turned her head to study her two sisters' faces.

"It's too late right now to go. We'd need a bit more time than what is left until morning."

"Can you figure out something to tell your parents?" Hannah said.

"Oh, dear." Lucy gasped and she suddenly felt sorry that she had called the figurehead her true mother. "I'll — I'll — I'll think of something. But I'd better get back now."

THE NETTED BIRD

ETTIE STOOD ON THE EDGE of the cove in a light drizzle. It had begun to rain shortly after the fireworks had finished. The moon had slipped away to another world . . . *another world*, she thought. Her pink-and-white-striped organdy dress hung limply around her ankles. There was no wind. The water was stippled with the rain, but she soon saw a kindling beneath the surface. *It's her*, she thought. How many times had she crouched behind the spruce to watch for Hannah's return? But the time for hiding was over. The time for truth had arrived. She would not divulge Hannah's secret. She would only tell her that she knew. She could not live a life of lies with Hannah.

Hannah broke through the water. She gasped when she saw Ettie and immediately ducked back down.

"Don't!" Ettie snapped. She marched right into the water, not bothering to take off her shoes. The hem of her skirt floated out around her.

"Look at your dress, Ettie!"

"Look at your tail!" Ettie's starry gray eyes widened.

She stood mesmerized, watching the flukes of Hannah's tail swaying back and forth in the water. The scales were so beautiful. She had never seen anything as beautiful.

"We can't stay here. Walk to the end of the point. I'll meet you there," Hannah said.

"All right," Ettie whispered.

It took less than three minutes to walk to the point at the end of the cove. When Ettie arrived, Hannah was already there.

"So when did you find out?" Hannah asked.

"Last summer just before the hurricane."

"You haven't told anybody?"

Ettie's face darkened. "Of course not. What do you take me for?" Her bottom lip began to tremble. "You're my best friend."

"Oh, Ettie!" Hannah moaned and reached to embrace her. Ettie was surprised how warm Hannah felt. The water was freezing cold, yet Hannah felt as if she had just stepped out of a warm tub, not Frenchman's Bay.

They were both crying now. Ettie's nose was running and she wiped it on her sleeve. "And I am your best friend," Hannah said.

Ettie pushed back and looked at her hard. "Are you sure, Hannah?" Ettie had an imperious little nose, even when it was runny, that could on occasion make her look very severe and vastly older than her years.

Hannah could not meet her eyes. "I want to be truthful, Ettie." Ettie had a terrible wrenching feeling inside her. *This must be how it feels when your heart breaks.* "There are others. Two . . . but they are not friends really."

"What do you mean?"

"They are my sisters."

"You have sisters? They are like you?" Hannah nodded. "But how . . . how did this happen? Mermaids are like fairy tales, aren't they?"

"No. I'm real. Touch me." She lifted her tail from the water. "Go ahead."

Hesitantly, Ettie reached out her hand and lightly ran her fingers over the scales. They felt silky, and when she took her hand away, she noticed a sprinkling of dust on her fingertips as if a rainbow had shed its colors.

"Don't worry," Hannah said. "It comes back — the colors."

"But how did this happen to you?"

"I was born this way."

"B-but where? Who are your parents?"

"It's a long story, Ettie, and so much of it is still a mystery to me."

"One of your sisters is that girl Lucy, isn't it? Lucy Snow. I played croquet with her."

"Yes, how did you guess?" Hannah asked with a note of fear in her voice.

"When she took off her hat . . . I mean her hair . . . her eyes."

"I hope no one else noticed," Hannah said.

"Of course not. No one notices servants, you know that." Hannah rolled her eyes but smiled. "So who's your other sister?"

"May Plum."

"Never heard of her."

Hannah grinned. "Of course not. She's a native. The lighthouse keeper's daughter on Egg Rock Island. And summer people never notice natives."

Ettie giggled. "Especially ones tucked away on islands in lighthouses." Then Ettie's face turned serious. "Where do you go when you swim?"

"Oh, just out . . . ," Hannah said vaguely.

Ettie felt she shouldn't push, but she was a child cursed with an overwhelming curiosity.

"Would you ever take me with you? I can swim really well, you know that."

"Oh, Ettie, this is a very different kind of swimming. We go deep sometimes into the coldest parts of the ocean, and the currents are strong."

"Don't you ever get cold?" Ettie asked.

Hannah shook her head. "You felt my skin. It's warm, right?"

"I know. How do you do that?"

"I don't do it. It's just the way I am."

"Are you ever scared when you're out there? I mean, there are big fish and storms and all sorts of things."

"I'm only ever scared on land, Ettie." The words seemed to hang in the air, spinning slowly. Like silent wind chimes they echoed in Ettie's mind.

"Me, too," Ettie whispered.

"Whatever do you mean, dear?"

Ettie looked far off. The dawn was just breaking. "It's a nasty place, isn't it — land?"

Hannah wasn't sure exactly what Ettie meant. Or perhaps she did and could not bear to believe that a child so young could have this view of the world. She took Ettie's hand and held it tight. "It will be all right, Ettie." For the first time, she felt Hannah was lying to her. Nothing was going to be all right. Ettie frowned. "Come on now, Ettie, it will be. You have a bright future."

"Girls like me have no futures. The future is more of a fairy tale than those in books. We just don't know it until we get there." There was almost a wild look in her eye, like a netted bird looking for escape.

Her desperate cynicism took Hannah's breath away.

SUMMER GAMES

"YOU KNOW WHAT I JUST HEARD, Lucy?" Her mother had sidled up to her as Lucy was testing the strength of her bow.

"What, Mother?"

"Letitia Aldrich, Mrs. Bannister's lovely niece, has just become engaged to a Russian prince. She's going to be a princess! Just imagine."

Lucy sighed.

"Why so glum, dear?" Marjorie Snow squeezed her daughter's hand, but tears had begun to well up in Lucy's eyes. "Lucy, is something the matter?"

Everything! she wanted to scream. "No, nothing. Please excuse me for a second."

"Where are you going, Lucy? The powder room is

the other way." But Lucy was halfway across the lawn by this time.

She looked behind her one final time before dashing out the gates of the Quoddy Club. She knew her parents would be furious, but she had to escape. She could no longer make small talk, and she couldn't stand to listen to it for another second.

❖   ❖   ❖

She was hurrying along the road, keeping her eyes down to hide her flushed cheeks from the villagers, when she bumped into someone heading the opposite direction. It was Phin.

His face reddened, and at first, she was convinced he was going to storm off without saying a word, but when he looked at Lucy, a flash of concern crossed his face. "Are you all right, Miss Snow?"

It all came rushing out. "Phin, forget that day on the path at Wyckmore. I was wretched to you. I am so sorry. I didn't know what was happening. I felt caught."

He raised his eyebrows. "Caught? Well, you're perfectly free now. I promise I won't bother you again." He started to walk off.

"Wait!" Lucy pleaded as she grabbed his elbow. "I'm not free. I'll never be free unless you forgive me. I'm so sorry."

"I don't know how they do things in New York, Miss Snow, but up here, we consider it bad manners to play games with people's feelings. Or perhaps that's just sport for you summer folk."

She recoiled as if his words had actually struck her, but then took a deep breath and stepped forward. "Don't call me summer folk," she said with more than a hint of anger in her voice. Her jaw began to tremble. "And please, please don't call me Miss Snow." She was close to sobbing. "It's not true, Phin. What you say. I do care about you. More than I've ever cared about anyone. You have to forgive me for being so foolish."

He stared at her for a moment and then flicked the bow hanging from her arm. "If I say no, are you going to shoot me?"

Lucy smiled for the first time, then sighed deeply. "The question is, How did I spend the whole morning without murdering the duke?" She laughed. "A homicidal cupid — perfect for an archery tournament."

"Murder. You were going to have to resort to murdering him?"

"I had to get away somehow."

Phin smiled and took her hand in his. "You look well, Lucy."

"I do?"

He nodded. "I can't explain it, but you look . . . well, just yourself but more."

She laughed. "How does one look more oneself?"

"Not really sure. But you do."

Lucy looked at him. "I think you might be the only person who knows what I really look like, who doesn't try to imagine me as something else."

Phin ran his finger along her cheek. "I couldn't imagine anything better."

Lucy cocked her head to the side. "You dream up ships for a living. Surely you could come up with *some* improvement."

He lowered his head and brushed his lips against hers. His kiss said it all.

❧   ❧   ❧

"You're a dear, Muffy," Lucy said when she met up with her at the entrance to the Quoddy Club, where they had planned to meet to appear as if they had been together.

"Well, I did my best. But, oh my Lord, here he comes now."

The duke was grinning. "Aah, you're back, Miss Snow."

"Not for long!" Muffy said brightly. Lucy looked at her, trying to disguise her surprise. "I have just engaged Miss Snow as a wedding advisor. She must come and look at my trousseau immediately. I need the honest opinion of a New Yorker." She gave an exaggerated sigh. "You know we women from Boston are known for our dowdiness."

"Oh, never!" the duke exclaimed. "But what about the archery tournament?"

"She can't, not today. Now come along, Lucy. We

have to hurry. Boynton is waiting with my trap."
She grabbed Lucy's arm and ushered her across
the lawn.

As soon as they climbed into the trap, Lucy
turned to her new friend. "Thank heavens, Muffy.
You are the best."

"Not quite."

"What do you mean?"

A cunning sparkle lit Muffy's cornflower blue
eyes. "I am not as selfless as you might think. Tell
me. Why did you simply have to get away? You have
a secret." Lucy stifled a shudder. *Which one?* "A
secret admirer whom you find more attractive than
the Duke of Crompton?" The color rose in Lucy's
cheeks. "Bull's-eye! Might I say? Come on now. Tell
me, please. Who is he?"

"You promise not to tell?"

"Of course I won't tell." Muffy looked at Lucy with
a level gaze. "I promise."

"He's . . . how — how to put it?"

"Put what?"

"You would consider him inappropriate."

"Who, Lucy? Who? I mean, is he married? A drunkard?"

"No, never. Phineas is not inappropriate in that way."

"Phineas! Phineas Heanssler, the young yacht designer?" Lucy nodded. Muffy sank back against the upholstered cushions of the trap. "Good Lord!"

"You see, I knew you would think that."

"Think what? That he's inappropriate? Not exactly. It's quite romantic, I suppose, and he is very hand-some. B-b-b-but . . ." Lucy had never heard Muffy stammer. She felt a dread rising.

"But what, Muffy? You don't approve?"

"It has nothing to do with approval, Lucy. It's just that it could be hard being in love with someone like that. I mean, his life is very different from yours." Lucy was thankful she did not say that he was differ-ent, that he was a native or that "his kind" was different, just his life. It seemed less judgmental. "I mean, do you think it is realistic?"

What was realistic anymore? If she told Muffy that every night she went into the sea and swam off with her skin turning to scales from the waist down and her legs fusing into a tail with flukes? Muffy must have read the anxiety that suddenly seemed to engulf Lucy.

"Look, Lucy, don't listen to me. In one sense, you're really lucky."

"Lucky? How? My parents would lock me up in the attic before they'd allow me to be seen with Phin."

"Don't you see? You have real freedom. I don't mean to be coarse, but if my father didn't have all this money . . . well."

"Well, what?"

"My parents are so worried about fortune hunters. And, in a sense, that is exactly what the Earl of Lyford is. He has no money, not like Daddy, but he has estates and a title. So therefore that counts."

"But you love him, don't you?"

"Well," she said slowly, "he is the dearest man. A true gentleman. But it's not passion. Not what you feel for Phineas. I can tell."

There was such resignation in Muffy's voice that

Lucy was left with a feeling of overwhelming sadness. There were so many questions that Lucy was sorely tempted to ask Muffy — Did she really think she should marry Lyford? Had she ever had a deep passion for someone, a true love?

Perhaps Muffy sensed Lucy's apprehension, for she began to talk with great animation.

"Lucy, I think my life will be just grand, so grand! We are to go to Rome for our honeymoon. And then it's the earl's custom to spend the spring in Paris every year, as he says England is so soggy that there is no real spring. And he knows so much about art. I don't know anything. But I'll be able to see it through his eyes and learn."

What about your own eyes? Lucy wanted to scream.

"It's really going to be fine ... so fine." Muffy reached out and patted Lucy's hand as if to reassure her.

❖   ❖   ❖

"Lucy, where have you been for the last hour?" Marjorie Snow rushed up as Lucy came into the cottage. "When I saw the duke at the Quoddy Club, he said you went off with Muffy Forbes."

"Yes, Mother, I did. I might be spending a great deal of time with Muffy."

Ever since Lucy had met her sisters and learned about their true mother, she found it difficult to look at her mother directly. She knew it was ridiculous, but she feared that Marjorie Snow would somehow detect a trace in her eyes, and Lucy did not want to hurt her adoptive mother. And that is how she now thought of Marjorie Snow — as her "adoptive mother" and not Mum. She felt guilty for this small perfidy and had gone out of her way to please Marjorie. She knew what she was about to tell her would be greeted with boundless joy.

"Really? Why is that, dear?"

"She has asked me to be one of her bridesmaids."

"Lucy!" Marjorie Snow's pale brown eyes grew as large as saucers. "Tell me it is true."

"Of course it's true, Mother. I guess you would say I have been 'taken up.'"

"You certainly have!" Marjorie Snow's high-pitched joyous exclamation drilled the air. "Stephen! Stephen!" she called. "Come out of your study and listen to this."

"What is it? What has so ruffled you up, Marjorie?"

"Tell him, Lucy. Tell him exactly what you told me . . . just the way you told me." Marjorie was fluttering her hands through the air as if conducting an invisible orchestra. "I want you to use the exact same words."

Lucy inhaled deeply. "I told mother that I would be spending more time with Muffy Forbes and she asked why and I replied . . ." Lucy could not believe how stupid this all sounded, but she glanced at her mother and saw the glow on her face, so she forged on. "It is because Muffy has asked me to be a bridesmaid."

"Oh my goodness!" Stephen said. "Lucy, our darling Lucy!" He came up and embraced her. Then he backed away while still clasping her hands. "Prettiest girl on the island."

What would you think if I told you there were two more almost identical to me? And we sometimes have tails. She almost giggled at the thought.

"Now, my dear," he continued, "do you remember what I was saying about Percy Wilgrew and the coast being clear?"

Lucy felt a dread welling up in her.

"Yes, Father, something about an entailment."

"Or lack thereof," her father replied. "Do you understand?"

"I understand that I have no money and that most of these titled Englishmen come over here looking for money so their poor old crumbling estates won't fall down around their ears and leave them standing in a heap of rubble."

"Lucy!" her mother gasped and her father's face had assumed a granite-like rigidity. He dropped her hands and stepped back from her.

"How dare you be so coarse as to talk about money?" His face darkened.

"How dare I?" Lucy's eyes blazed like green fire. "That's all anyone ever talks about here. Money. How much the Bellamy yacht cost. How Muffy Forbes's father is giving her one hundred thousand dollars a year, and how the wedding itself is rumored to cost almost ten thousand dollars. How the Van Wycks are

227

ordering a yacht ten feet longer and therefore at least twenty thousand dollars more than the Bellamys' yacht."

"Now how do you know that?" barked her father.

Lucy realized that she had said too much. The only reason she knew this detail was because of Phineas.

"I — I — I just heard it around the Quoddy Club," she stammered. "As I said, everyone talks about money." She inhaled deeply and her eyes filled with tears. "Why would you ever think Percy Wilgrew would want me? We simply don't have the money."

"I don't think he is looking merely for money!" Her father raised his voice to the brimstone level that he always criticized in ministers from certain denominations less elegant than his own. "Lucy, it's position. His family has close ties with the archbishop of Canterbury." Her father was now roaring.

"So what now?" Lucy roared back. "You're going to trade me for the chance to be the archbishop of Canterbury?" With that she turned and ran from the cottage. From the corner of her eye, she could see her mother collapsing in a chair and burying her face in her hands.

"Don't worry, my dear," she heard her father saying. "Just a bit of youthful rebellion. She'll be back."

THE STARRY CROWN

"**ALL RIGHT NOW,** lift up and set your flukes just on the crest line of the wave; dig in a bit with your left one. That's how you steer."

"Eeeyiii!" Lucy shouted, and catching the edge of her other fluke in the curl, she flipped over and slid down the side of the wave.

Laughing, she swam back toward the ledge to wait for another wave.

"That was good!" Hannah said.

"Good? Don't be crazy. I only rode it for what, five seconds."

"That's four seconds longer than I did in my first storm. Come on, you'll get better."

It had all begun when she found the note in the

cave that morning — the morning after the fight with her parents. It was from May.

Storm coming tonight. Meet us on Simon's Ledge. M

She was going to be late, for her parents had taken forever to go to bed. But as soon as she was sure they were quite sound asleep, she was out the door and in the water. She swam fast and hard through the churning seas, but already she was feeling the thrill that May and Hannah had described. For tonight they were going to teach her to surf.

Within another few attempts, Lucy was riding the waves as well as her sisters.

"Look! Look! Look at her go, May!" Hannah yelled jubilantly.

Lucy was skimming through the barrel, the hollow space of a breaking wave between the face of the wave and the crest as it curled over. As the waves moved into shallower water, the bottom of the wave decreased in speed, and the top started to spill forward and break. Lucy began to understand the rhythm and structure of the waves. Her entire being thrilled as she swooped through the watery tunnel.

She felt as if she were coursing through the very heart of the sea. Its roar filled her ears, the crushing sound of the water throbbed through her like the rush of blood through an artery. When the rain had ceased and the sky cleared, there was one moment that Lucy would never forget as long as she lived. The barrel had almost closed, leaving an opening like a peephole that framed the sky, and within that frame, seven stars rose in a soft curve scooping the night. It glowed like an upside-down tiara in the August night, and Lucy couldn't help but think she had been crowned some sort of wild salt princess of the waves.

"Do you see it?" May asked breathlessly, pointing at the constellation of seven stars. "Look just up there now that the clouds have cleared off." The three sisters were drifting lazily on their backs between the wide troughs of waves.

"Yes," said Lucy, "the one that looks like the upside-down tiara. I caught a glimpse when I was skimming through the barrel."

"That's what it is exactly. A crown. It's called the

Corona Borealis — the Northern Crown. It's easiest to see in August. But even then, it can be hard to see."

"How do you know so much about the stars, May?" She saw her two sisters exchange nervous glances.

Then May turned to Lucy. "I have a beau, May. His name is Hugh — Hugh Fitzsimmons — and he is an astronomer."

"And I, too," Hannah said. "It's a long story, Lucy. Maybe we should swim back to the cave. There is still time before dawn."

❧ ❧ ❧

"Stannish Whitman Wheeler! He is your beau, Hannah?" Hannah nodded. "He's famous. Muffy Forbes is having her portrait painted by him."

"He's not just famous, Lucy. He's mer." Then she added quickly, "Or was mer."

This was almost too much for Lucy to absorb. "Was? Is?" She turned to May. "And yours — the astronomer. He is mer, too?"

"No," May said, shaking her head. She seemed slightly wistful.

"But does he know about you?"

"Yes," May said, and this time she smiled a bit.

Lucy put her hands to her eyes and pressed as if to keep back the tears. "I have someone I love dearly and though he is not mer, he knows the ways of the sea."

"You do?" both May and Hannah said at once.

"Phineas Heanssler," Lucy said softly.

"Phineas!" they both exclaimed.

"Yes, but he knows nothing about . . . this secret life of mine."

"It might be all right," May said.

"Or it might not," Hannah replied.

Lucy lifted her eyes to Hannah. "Why do you say to that, Hannah?"

"The Laws of Salt." She spoke softly.

"Laws of Salt? What are the Laws of Salt?"

"You'll learn," May said.

"It's not exactly learning. You begin to feel them. Unless someone like Stannish tells them to you for your own sake." A bitterness had crept into Hannah's voice that Lucy had never heard before.

"Feel them?" she asked.

"When we take you to the wreck of the *Resolute* and when you see the figurehead of our mother. You will feel them, and start to know them."

"But how will they help me with Phineas?"

"They don't help you, exactly. They just make you feel or know your true nature better, I think," May said.

Hannah sighed. "You see, I think that Stannish . . . well, Stannish gave up the sea for the land. He was older than we are."

"For what? Another love? Another girl?" Lucy asked.

"No, painting. Art."

"Can't he have both?"

Hannah shook her head grimly. "He can't go back now. He would" — she hesitated — "most likely drown."

"Drown," Lucy repeated, as if the word were from a foreign language. She would never drown. It was unimaginable.

"We must take you to the *Resolute*. Then you will begin to understand."

23

THE BRIDESMAID ADVISES

THERE WAS NEVER a more ardent bridesmaid than Lucy. It was not merely because of the opportunity it offered her to pursue her secret lives but indeed Lucy had grown genuinely fond of Matilda Forbes. Since Lucy was artistically gifted, she often sketched out with her watercolors or colored pencils ideas she had for the wedding. Muffy's mother, Bessie, had one framed as a keepsake of her daughter's wedding year. Both girls had served on the altar guild committee, and inspired by the wildflowers they collected, Muffy had decided she must have such a bouquet as a bride.

"But how?" Lucy asked. "Your wedding is in late October and the summer wildflowers will be gone."

"Oh, we have wonderful greenhouses. I'll ask the gardener about raising some."

"But they're wild," Lucy said. "I'm not sure if something wild can be raised in a greenhouse."

"Well, we can try!" Muffy said brightly.

It still seemed wrong to Lucy, so she decided to come up with a more appropriate choice for the season.

Two days later, there was a knock on the front door of the Snows' house as Lucy was sketching a bouquet for Muffy.

"Come in!" Lucy called out.

"Lucy, that is so common. Just because we don't have a full-time maid here doesn't mean you let just anyone in," her mother said as she rose and went to the door.

"Yes?" Lucy heard her mother say in a slightly querulous tone. "What do you want?"

"Oh, Mother, it's Boynton from the Forbes cottage," Lucy said, leaning over from her perch on the couch.

"Yes, ma'am, a note for Miss Lucy from Miss Matilda."

Lucy took the envelope and opened it.

> *Dear girl, please come right away.*
> *Need your advice on bridal veil.*
> *Affectionately,*
> *MF*

Lucy smiled.

"Of course, Boynton. Tell her I'll be right along."

"I can give you a lift if you'd like to come now. I've got the trap."

"Yes, just let me get my shawl and hat."

"Lucy, do you think it's proper?" Marjorie asked icily as Boynton walked down the front path.

"What, Mother? Muffy needs me."

"Yes, but a servant just showing up like that? In those coveralls, not liveried. In Newport, according to the duke, every servant has specially designed livery and instead of mere traps, people like Mrs. Vanderbilt and the Drexels all have phaetons, according to Percy."

Lucy mustered as much patience as possible

before she replied. "Mother, this is not Newport. It's Maine, and if Percy Wilgrew, the Duke of Crompton, thinks Newport is better, let him go there."

"Now, don't be that way."

"What way?"

"You're always so critical of Percy. And by the way, we are to have luncheon with him, so don't be late."

"Where?"

"At the Abenaki."

"For how long?"

"What do you mean for how long? As long as luncheon takes. Do be nice to him," she said with a sigh.

"Mother, I think I have been very nice. Extra nice, as a matter of fact." Since the nasty quarrel with her parents, Lucy had made an effort to be less confrontational with Percy Wilgrew. She had been civil and even cordial. Regretting how she had snapped at her mother, she turned to her and gently said, "Of course I'll be at luncheon. Don't worry."

"Oh, Lucy, you're just so dear, so special. Your father and I only want the best for you."

Special, Lucy thought. *If she only knew!*

What would her mother do? The thought chilled her to the bone.

"You see, it's supposed to fit like this and then the veil will flow out from the back!" Muffy stood before an oval mirror in her mother's boudoir. Her mother's maid was adjusting the diamond tiara on Muffy's dark brown hair, which recalled the seven stars in the Corona Borealis that Lucy had seen that night through the barrel of the wave. "I think Tiffany's reset them perfectly. Don't you?" she said, turning to Lucy.

Lucy did not know what to say. She was hardly an expert in jewels. But in truth she felt that the jewels looked better set in the sky. The tiara appeared too big for Muffy's small head. But perhaps with the veil, they would not seem so overpowering.

Lucy answered cautiously, "Yes, the diamonds are quite lovely. Where will the veil attach?"

"Right back here." Bessie stood up and pointed to

small silver loops at the back of the tiara. "Marisa, will you go fetch the veils?"

"Certainly, madam."

Two minutes later, the maid was back, her arms embracing what appeared to be a huge mound of clouds.

"This is our first choice," Muffy said, putting on a lace veil. Lucy thought it made her look top heavy and did little to reduce the rather monumental feeling of the tiara. She wished they would simply forget about the tiara with the seven diamonds, but she knew this was not an option. After twenty minutes of trying on at least five different veils, some of tulle, some of Alençon lace, some waltz length, some fingertip or elbow length, and some cathedral length, Lucy sighed. "I have an idea, but . . . but I'm not sure if it's ever done."

"We certainly don't want anything too revolutionary," Bessie Forbes said.

"What if Muffy wore two veils?"

"Two veils!" the mother and daughter exclaimed.

"Yes. First the Alençon lace that is shoulder length and then the tulle that is waltz length."

"Well, I suppose we could try it." Bessie Forbes's voice wavered slightly as if she were considering a life-threatening decision.

Yet two minutes later, everyone in the room was gasping with delight.

"I think it looks nice," Muffy said.

"Nice! It's brilliant. Lucy, you are a genius! Muffy, your father will be so pleased. He was, in his old Boston way, hesitant about the tiara. Thought it was a bit *de trop*, as the French say."

Lucy couldn't have agreed more with Mr. Forbes, but smiled. Bessie Forbes squealed and jumped up to hug her. Muffy stood to the side quietly wrapped in the cloud of tulle. The sweeping waltz-length veil billowing out over the shorter lace one somehow did balance the tiara. Lucy peered through the gauzy mist of the veil to find Muffy's very still and utterly expressionless face. She could not help but recall the resignation in Muffy's voice when she had spoken so candidly about her future husband. *"He is the dearest man. But it's not passion."* And this wedding did not seem to be a wedding. This bride did not seem to be a bride, and the voluminous mist of fabric was perhaps more a shroud than a veil.

"Yes," she said in a small voice. "It seems quite lovely this way. Thanks, Lucy. Thanks so much."

"I'm happy I could be of help, but it's almost one, and Mother expects me at the Abenaki for luncheon."

"You were of more than just help. You are a lifesaver!" Bessie Forbes exclaimed. This overstatement struck Lucy as deeply ironic. "Do tell your mother that you are the best bridesmaid my daughter could ask for!" Mrs. Forbes effused.

Lucy just laughed. She would tell her but in private. She did not want to bring up the subject of brides or weddings with Percy Wilgrew present.

As she was leaving, Muffy whispered. "Is you-know-who going to be there?"

"Naturally."

"Now, girls, who is 'you-know-who'?" Bessie asked.

"Percy Wilgrew, Duke of Crompton," Muffy replied quickly.

"Oh, he is so delightful, a real charmer. Do you know that —" she began.

"Mother! You've told this story a million times."

"Well, it's a *wonderful* story and only Percy could have pulled it off."

"What is it?" Lucy felt she had to ask.

"He met Mrs. Astor, the Newport one. *The* Mrs. Astor," she emphasized so it would be clear that it was not the Bar Harbor one, who she seemed to think was a tarnished inferior metal next to the real fourteen-karat gold one. "You know she is normally so proper and private, but she was so fascinated by Percy that he actually got her to dine in public at Sherry's. It was in all the papers the next day. You see, she is such a grande dame that she never had dined in a restaurant. Rather like Queen Victoria, I suppose. She never dines out. It was a landmark event when Mrs. Astor walked into Sherry's accompanied by Percy."

"Really?" Lucy replied, trying to feign interest. She smiled to herself. Phin created entire ships pulled from the depths of his imagination, and Percy's greatest accomplishment was convincing a rich old lady to go out to dine.

❧   ❧   ❧

"And she dined out. The diners at Sherry's couldn't have been more surprised if Queen Victoria had walked in."

It was positively eerie. Lucy felt as if she had entered some infinite loop of conversation, a perfect echo of the conversation she had just left, almost word for word. The Duke of Crompton was holding forth at a tea table on the veranda of the Abenaki Club with several ladies, including Lucy's mother, along with Isabel Schuyler and Melda Gibson, a proper old maid who was a distant and impoverished relative of Isabel's.

"Oh my goodness!" Marjorie Snow slapped her plump cheek in amazement at the story the duke was telling.

"Lucy, dear, so glad you came. Dear Percy, you must repeat the story for Lucy."

And so he did. Lucy tried to appear as attentive

and engaged as possible. She asked a few questions. She was trying, she thought. She hoped her mother noticed.

"And how was your visit with Muffy? Muffy trusts her, as does her mother, Bessie, implicitly." She looked over at the duke.

"I'm sure they do, and might I hazard a guess that your visit had something to do with the peacock diamonds?"

"Peacock? Is that what they call them?"

"Oh, yes. They were said to belong to the emperor of China."

How Percy Wilgrew knew the reason for her visit defied Lucy's imagination, but she did not want to give him the satisfaction of asking. She turned to him and smiled very sweetly. "Yes, that in fact was the reason for my visit. They have had the stones reset for a tiara to which her veil will be attached. I, of course, know so little about jewels. We have none," she said distinctly. "After all, we are a parson's family." She could feel her mother wince at the word *parson.*

"Prissy has lovely jewels," Marjorie Snow added. There was a tinge of desperation in her voice as she raced down the conversational field like a player trying to recover a fumbled ball.

The duke continued seamlessly, as if he had not heard the jewel remark at all. "You know, it has always been my thinking that Bessie Forbes, really one of the most stylish women here, or anywhere for that matter, would find herself much more comfortable in Newport. She is so very, very . . . Newport!" He then turned to Lucy and beamed. "You are in a very special position, Lucy. To be selected as a bridesmaid — what an honor."

"Yes. I am very pleased, for Muffy is a lovely girl. I shall miss her when she moves to England," Lucy replied demurely.

"Oh, you shan't at all. You shall visit her, and Lyford Hall is quite near to Ashleigh Manor. It will all be so convenient."

Convenient? Lucy thought but dared not ask.

As lunch finished, Lucy rehearsed the little speech that was to be her excuse for not accompanying her mother home, and precluded Percy from accompanying her anywhere. Muffy loved nothing more that devising pretenses for Lucy's secret meetings with Phineas.

"I am afraid I have a very special assignment to complete for Muffy. All I shall tell you is it has to do with certain garments for the bridesmaids. So I must be on my way to speak with a certain seamstress. All very top secret."

"Oh, Lucy, bless you, child. What would the Forbeses do without you?"

"I can't imagine," Percy said. "And by the way, now that the Van Wycks are building a boat larger than the Bellamys', I understand that the Forbeses are also considering one even bigger than the Van Wycks'."

"Yes," Marjorie said. "I heard that as well. Did Muffy say anything to you, darling?"

"No," Lucy replied. "We were concentrating on bridal matters."

"Well, I have it on good authority that the Heanssler boatyard is said to be contracted," the duke offered.

Percy turned to Lucy and said almost confidentially, "It's really going to be quite amazing, I hear." He turned to the others. "I think the royal family might be envious of the Forbeses. You know, the Prince of Wales just commissioned a new yacht. I don't think his mother was too keen on it."

"Why not?" Lucy asked.

"She's rather frugal actually. It seems quite ridiculous, but that's the way she is. And getting more so in her dotage."

"I understand that she still dresses in mourning for her late husband, Prince Albert."

"Yes. They were very devoted."

His remark struck Lucy as odd. "Aren't most married couples?"

Marjorie Snow shot Lucy a glance as if to demand, "*Why must you always question so?*"

"Well, yes, but the prince has been dead for years now, decades."

"But if she still mourns him, perhaps dressing that way makes her feel most comfortable."

"Yes, but as a monarch, her duty is to her country.

It casts rather a pall, you know. When you have a title, you cannot think just of yourself but of the dominion of which you are the protector. Even mourning can become an indulgence when there is a realm to consider."

"An indulgence, Your Grace?" Lucy turned to the duke in wonder.

"Quite right," Marjorie Snow murmured. "Stephen often counsels grieving widows or widowers that it is God's will that one get on with life."

Lucy continued speaking despite the fact that her mother had given her a kick under the table. "I am having a hard time understanding how what the queen wears or how long she mourns really has to do with the average British citizen like yourself."

The duke winced, then chuckled slightly. "Average, Lucy? I hardly think of myself as average."

"I meant no offense, sir." She could feel waves of discomfort radiating from her mother, but she could not stop herself from speaking out. The others at the table had fallen silent. Their heads swiveled first to Lucy and then to the duke, as if they were watching a tennis match. Yet she was not embarrassed at all. His sense of superiority with more than an irksome tinge of entitlement was insufferable. If he knew how "average" she truly was — at least in one sense — he would most likely dismiss her at once. She only wished she had the courage to tell him that her mother's fanciful stories of their connections to Aunt Prissy were just that. But she dared not. They would all look like fools, then.

"I know you meant no offense. Nor did I." He bent his head toward her slightly and she caught a whiff of hair oil. "As I was saying" — his voice resonated with a forced cheeriness — "the Forbes yacht will be even grander than the Van Wyck one."

Lucy was dying to say, "Yes, I spent quite a bit of time in the master bedroom," but wisely held her tongue. She began to make her excuses to leave, and was slightly alarmed when the duke insisted on escorting her from the table.

"These island people," Percy continued as they stood on the veranda of the Abenaki Club, "are quite clever, you know."

"You sound surprised, Percy." It was the first time she had used his Christian name, and she saw his eyes dance with delight.

"Well, you know, they aren't . . ." He seemed to search for a word.

"Aren't what?" Lucy looked at him closely. Her chin jutted forward a bit. "Or are they just average?"

Percy Wilgrew scratched at the side of his head as if this required a great deal of thought. "They don't have the advantages that some of us do. Our kind."

"I'm not sure I take your meaning?" she said softly. She was feeling quite unsettled with this talk.

"You know."

"I assure you, sir, I am not your kind, not in the least."

"I am not just talking about titles, Miss Snow. Yes, I am a duke with a title, which is a custom in England and not here. But of course it is," he laughed, "easily remedied. Such is the case with Matilda Forbes and the Earl of Lyford. She will soon be a countess." Lucy could not believe what she was hearing. He was actually dangling titles in front of her like a sideshow barker at a carnival. "I believe that your mother's dear cousin Priscilla Bancroft has visited Lyford Hall. As I understand it, Lyford Hall bears some resemblance to White Oaks, where you were practically raised."

Practically raised? My mother's cousin? What had her mother been saying?

"Aunt Prissy?" Lucy said vaguely.

"Yes, I believe that's the nickname your mother called her by. She is your godmother, correct?"

"Yes," Lucy answered numbly, but she had fastened her eyes on her mother, who was engaged in an animated discussion with Muffy Forbes's father. What yarns was her mother spinning? she wondered.

"I really must be on my way." Lucy turned to walk away. She was about to run.

"Please don't go."

"I'm quite late already."

He reached out to grab her hand and caught the cuff of her dress. There was a rip and the sleeve tore halfway off.

"Oh, I am so sorry. I didn't mean to." He was still holding the cuff. Lucy looked at her bare arm for several seconds. This was the same arm that had pulled her so powerfully through the water. She looked into the duke's eyes.

"Sir, make no mistake. I assure you once again, I am not your kind."

THE PEARL BUTTON

PERCY WAITED in the shadows of the carriage house of the Abenaki Club, which afforded him a perfect view of the drive.

Why has she turned left, away from town? What possible bridesmaid's errand could take her that way? Percy Wilgrew thought. He would get to the bottom of this. By hook or by crook he was determined to get to the bottom of it. He had to. He had no choice. Every week, a cable arrived from his mother outlining the dire straits that had befallen Ashleigh Manor, the ancestral home that had been in their family since granted by Henry VII to Michael Percy in 1487.

The road out of the village of Bar Harbor was a winding one and, thankfully, lined with thick stands of trees. It was easy for him to follow Lucy unde-tected. He watched as she cut across the field. On the far side were the burnt-out ruins of the Grantmore Hotel. She seemed to be running now. He would have to walk quickly to keep pace.

Five minutes later, he reached the ruins, but Lucy seemed to have disappeared. Then he spied a path that led into the woods behind the hotel.

Percy Wilgrew heard them before he saw them. Heard the pronounced breathing, the rustle of leaves and twigs breaking. He closed his eyes and leaned against a tree. *So this is her bridesmaid's errand!* He crept closer, careful not to make a sound himself. He first caught sight of her hair, loose around her shoul-ders. Someone was embracing her passionately. Who was it? He waited. Patience was one of the duke's vir-tues. But soon the fellow got up and brushed himself off. He turned and would have looked directly into Percy Wilgrew's eyes if it had not been for the thick trunk of the ancient oak. But Percy had seen him. *That boatyard boy!* He could hardly believe it. *She spurns me, spurns a title for that?* Percy felt a rage flare within him. He would not be made a fool of. Never!

The Duke of Crompton was not only a patient man but a careful one. He planned. He strategized. He continued to watch, perfectly still. Lucy's shawl lay on the ground. The sleeves of her dress fell off her shoulders to expose a shocking expanse of skin. She raised her bare arms to twist up her hair. He was hypnotized by the slow languorous movement of her arms as she wound her hair. It was horrible and yet he could not tear his eyes from her. She was dangerous. She needed to be destroyed.

Percy wasn't sure how much time passed before Lucy pressed her lips against the shipbuilder's one final time and led him away, smiling. When he was sure they had left, Percy walked over to the patch of moss where Lucy and Phineas had lain entwined and spied something glistening on top of the moss. A pink pearl button. He bent over and picked it up. Folding his hand around it tightly, he smiled into the shadows of the forest. *This will be easy*, he thought. Now he had all he needed.

UNDERWATER TEARS

It was as May and Hannah had told her. She felt it as soon as they swam out of the current — an inexorable pull stronger than the stream that had sped them to the shoals. Like iron filings toward a magnet she was aware of every fiber of her body and mind driving toward this place that was unknown and yet so peculiarly familiar.

They had left for the shoals at dawn. Each of the sisters had made excuses to be gone for the day. Lucy had once again invoked her bridesmaid's duties, though she had told Muffy it was something to do with Phineas. Hannah had worked two extra days and therefore arranged for a day off. May had the easiest time of all. She merely told her father that Hugh was coming up and they planned to hike Mount Abenaki, which they often did. Her father, Gar, wished her a good day and said not to worry about the lighthouse chores. He'd be fine on his own.

Hannah and May had never been to the wreck during the daytime, and today was particularly sunny. They usually saw the hulk of the sunken ship through the reflected light of the moon. But now the shadowy depths were latticed with sunlight and hovering amidst the shafts like a golden angel, a sea angel. Lucy saw a face so like her own, so like her sisters that she stopped swimming for a moment and held still in the water. Then she slipped slowly through the shafts of light toward the figurehead that extended from the bow of the ship.

"Mum," she whispered in the watery language. Reaching out with her arms, she embraced the slender wooden neck. *If only you were flesh,* she thought. *And not hard wood.* What had it been like to be held by her, cradled in her arms?

She was not sure how long she had been holding

her, but she felt stirrings in the water as her sisters approached.

She turned to May and Hannah. "How does one cry underwater?"

"Look," Hannah said softly. "Look at the figure-head's chin — the small dimple is the same as ours." Hannah touched Lucy's chin as Lucy looked up at the face of her mother.

"Do we know her name?" Lucy asked.

Hannah and May shook their heads.

"How do you think she came to be on this ship? Were we born here?"

The girls shook their heads again. "These questions," May began, "seem almost impossible to answer. We have pondered all of them. It is all so mysterious. We can only half guess at the answers. We know the name of the captain. Captain Walter Lawrence."

"Do you believe he could have been our father?" Lucy asked.

"Maybe," Hannah said.

"Was he mer?"

May shrugged. "It's really hard to know much for sure," she said.

"But the mystery in a way begins with this ship. The *Resolute*. We'll show you through her," Hannah said. "We're always looking for clues. Something to tell us more about our mother and the captain."

They swam through a rent in the vast hull.

"This is the captain's quarters," May said as they swam close to an upturned navigation desk.

"It's where we found the scallop shell comb, the shell like May's. She said I could have it since she already had one. Maybe we can find another one for you."

"If not I know where we can dive for one. Same place I found mine. A ledge down deep near Matinicus Rock."

But Lucy was not paying attention. She had found something else. The small cubbyholes above the bed.

"There's a chambered nautilus in one of those. He hates being disturbed," Hannah said.

"But what's this?" Lucy asked, drawing out a rock fragment.

"Oh, that! We almost forgot," Hannah answered.

"It's lovely," Lucy said as she held the fragment up to a ray of sunlight and studied the feathery design.

"We think it's a keepsake of our mother's," May said.

"So why didn't you take it with you? I mean, if it is our mother's keepsake, wouldn't you want it? And couldn't it be a clue?"

May and Hannah looked at each other, genuinely puzzled. "I think perhaps we were waiting for you," May said slowly. "We can take it back to the cave now."

"Its design looks like a broken flower — a lily," Lucy said, quietly tracing it with her fingertip. "It must be a fossil. I've seen them in the natural history museum in New York, just like this."

"Really?" May said. "You've seen true fossils?"

"I'd love to go to a museum," Hannah added. "Never been to one myself."

"Me, neither," May said.

"But you know," Lucy continued, looking at it more closely, "it's not just that it looks like a lily. There is a flow to it. It could almost be a picture of a current. The marks look like water streaming."

Something stirred in Lucy's memory, a recent memory. "It reminds me of something else as well."

"What?" Hannah asked.

"Something I've seen or heard or read about."

"Or dreamed about?" Hannah said.

"Maybe. But I just can't remember it right now."

"It'll come to you," May said. "But we'd best be swimming back now."

As Lucy swam, she thought of the sea-polished face of the figurehead, her mother. There were dim traces of the colors that had been — the rosiness of her plump lips, a thin veil of green in her eyes hinted at a deeper green scrubbed by the sea, and the shadow of what once had been the brilliant red of her hair. It took very little imagination to see what had been there nearly eighteen years before. Lucy grasped the rock fragment tightly in her fist and began wondering not so much about the color of her mother's eyes or her face but her voice. It was then that the memory came back. Echoes of another voice — that of Dr. Forsythe, whom she had listened to on that spring morning in the Museum of Natural History.

"A man in a sealskin boat, enshrouded in his seal-skin parka. A seal man, they began to call these people who came across the sea with not a mortal wound, a trace of violence, but who had died in the icy embrace of the winter sea when blown from their course. . . . The selkie legends, the mythological shape-shifting creatures, seal folk, who are said to be seals in the sea but humans upon the land."

"A kind of mermaid?"

"Lucy are you talking to yourself?" May had swum up beside her.

"Selkies!" Lucy said. "But we're not seals."

"Whatever are you talking about?" Hannah asked. "Have you remembered something? The rock — you know what it reminded you of?"

"Yes, in a sense. It's all coming together for me. And it's not a dream!"

"No?" May asked.

"No, it's as you say. The Laws of Salt," Lucy replied.

THE OTHER HALF

ACROSS THE SEA on Barra Head, the scripture of the Laws of Salt began to stir in another's veins. Avalonia went to the notch in the cave wall where she kept her half of the rock. She peered at the fragment and began to weep as a flood of joy mingled with profound sorrow swirled through her, spinning like the waters of the Gyre of Corry.

They have found one another. She closed her eyes tight and thought of that day so many years ago when she and her sister, Laurentia, had each found the halves of the rock.

Then their mother had told them the story as she set the two rock fragments on the beach and fitted them together. "They call these sea lilies and sometimes feather stars. They are very ancient, from the time before time."

The sweep of the feather star design, however, looked exactly like the course of the Avalaur current for which the two girls, Avalonia and Laurentia, had been named. Sailors were careful to give it a wide berth, for there were tales of how it lured the unwary into its deathly vortex. For mer folk, the Avalaur current did not spell death but life, a renewal with a mystical link to the secret threads of their origin and their destiny. And thus the Laws of Salt began to stream through their veins as salt through the ocean.

"Now you see," said their mother as she held up the two rock fragments, "how special it is that these two pieces of the rock were found here by you two sisters."

"What does it mean, Mum?" Laurentia asked.

"It means that through life you shall always be linked, but even in death you shall never be completely separated."

Now all these years later, Avalonia clasped the rock in her hand. It was a clasp that seemed to stretch across the vastness of the ocean that separated her from her three nieces — Laurentia's daughters. *When will they come? When will they come?* She took down the clàrsach and, plucking the strings, began to sing.

Come home, come home to Barra Head
I'll show you the Gyre of Corry
Come home, come home, sisters three
I long to stroke your heads.

At this moment, as the girls swam into the cave, each one felt a sonorous thrum rising within her. It was as if a note had been struck and an ancient music began to flood through their beings. They looked at one another, their eyes bright with anticipation.

It was Lucy who spoke first. "I think our next long swim must be a very long one."

"Why do you say that?" May asked.

"Because we must swim across the Atlantic Ocean."

"But where to?" Hannah asked, her eyes widening.

"To the Hebrides, I think. For that is where our mother came from. It was what I was trying to remember when I first saw this rock." She held out her hand and traced the sinuous curves of the sea lily.

"And now you remember?" Hannah asked.

"Yes." So Lucy began to tell her sisters the story she had heard at the Museum of Natural History.

And when she had finished, May was the first to speak. "And though we are not seals but mer, we are all creatures of both land and sea, and over there, some of our kin wait for us?"

"Yes, I do believe it is so," Lucy spoke quietly.

CUT!

"**I JUST DON'T UNDERSTAND IT.**" Marjorie Snow was reading the note that had just been delivered. "Elena Hazlitt asked us both two weeks ago if we were free for the opera. And now she writes that she has made a horrendous mistake and their box is full. Stephen, do you understand?"

"Perhaps, my dear, it was one of the more racy operas, and she felt it wasn't appropriate for a clergyman to be seen in attendance."

"True," Marjorie replied. "What's the one about those scandalous artists in Paris?"

"*La Bohème?*" Lucy offered.

"That's the one!" Her mother put one finger to her temple and tapped it. It was almost as if she were trying to cram one more thought into her somewhat overcrowded brain.

Lucy often thought of her mother's mind as a small tenement building, the kind one saw on Orchard Street on the Lower East Side where she often accompanied her father, for he had a favorite cobbler there, Jacob Hurwitz. Lucy was fascinated by all the little shadowy corridors and the bombardment of cooking odors that seeped out from every door. Children ran willy-nilly all over the place. Doors constantly slamming, babies screaming, people arguing. It was an incoherent little universe, chaotic and impenetrable, and she gasped in disbelief when she saw two men wrestling with a steamer trunk as another family newly arrived with half a dozen children trailed behind. She could not imagine how another human being could be stuffed into the building. This was the picture that came to mind as she saw her mother insistently tapping the side of her head.

"Yes, *La Bohème*. All those seedy artists living together without benefit of clergy, no doubt. But the main character, the girl — she died, right?"

"Yes, Mimi the seamstress. She died," Lucy said.

"So there," Marjorie said.

"What do you mean, 'so there'?" Lucy asked.

"So she died. She was punished. So it is not a completely immoral opera."

Lucy simply did not know how to respond. She had had too much on her mind since the swim to the wreck of the *Resolute*. She and her sisters were determined to make the much longer swim, across the Atlantic to the Outer Hebrides, which was almost a three-thousand-mile journey. Not one of the three sisters knew what kind of excuse they could come up with to cover such a long absence. And then there was the question that none dared to speak. Would it be a mere visit or would they be gone forever?

"Oh, and, Lucy, I do feel that the celadon mousseline gown is the one you should wear to the tea dance this afternoon. You know, in Newport . . ."

But Lucy had wandered off to her bedroom.

Mrs. Sterling Van Wyck's prominent nose cut across the tented lawn like a racing sloop through the waves. She appeared to be heading directly toward where Marjorie Snow and Lucy had just entered.

"Those lilies she sent for the altar last Sunday were so exquisite." She leaned in toward Lucy. "Though her ringlets are a bit" — she hesitated — "*de trop* for a woman of her age. But she is so very handsome."

Mrs. Van Wyck was a scant four or five feet away. "Oh, Mrs. Van Wyck, it was so generous of you to donate those simply beautiful astral lilies, particularly as they must be the prize of your late August bloom."

But Cornelia Van Wyck suddenly vaporized. One second she had been feet from them, and the next gone. Marjorie Snow stood frozen as she felt a gathering cold pressing in upon her. The first loom of fog, like the swarthy gray mass that materialized on the horizon so many mornings. The fog would advance inexorably and, within minutes, swallow everything in a cold, damp impenetrable shroud.

What had just occurred was death. A kind of death she had heard of — *being cut* — in which one did not bleed, and yet she felt as though she were hemorrhaging. She had heard of people in society being cut, but never clergy. *Why?* The question shrieked in her brain. This bloodless act was the most lethal social injury one could suffer.

"Mother, is something wrong?" Lucy grew alarmed as her mother suddenly looked terribly pale.

Marjorie turned to her daughter. Had she not noticed the snub? *Impossible!*

"I'm not feeling well. I think I'll go home."

"I'll go with you."

"You mustn't. Your father will take me."

"No, Mother, I can. Remember, Father isn't here yet."

"Oh, no, look who's coming over to chat. The duke." Thank goodness someone still wanted to speak with them. A spark of hope flickered within Marjorie Snow's breast.

"Ah, just the girl I wanted to see. Miss Snow."

"How lovely to see you," Marjorie Snow said in a quavering voice. But the flicker grew dim. *Miss Snow?*

"I believe this is yours?" He held out his hand. In it was a pale pink pearl button.

"Oh my God!" Lucy said hoarsely.

"Lucy, is that a button from your —" Marjorie Snow could not utter the word.

"Yes, I found it," the duke said as a smirk like a fat worm crawled across his face.

"Where?" Lucy asked weakly, and felt her mother sway and clutch her arm.

"In the woods behind the Grantmore Hotel."

"W-w-what . . ." Her mother's lips seemed to wobble while it searched for the shape of the next word. "What was she doing there?"

"Perhaps you should ask your daughter," the duke said, turned, and walked away quickly.

Lucy would never know how exactly she navigated her mother out of the tent. They had not gone far when Gus Bellamy rushed up to them.

"I'll drive you back. I have our trap here." It was not a question.

"Gus . . . Gus, what is happening?" Lucy asked.

"I'll tell you" — he looked at Marjorie Snow — "I'll

tell you later." He bent over and whispered quickly in her ear, "Not in front of your mother."

"Yes, of course," Lucy replied, and cast a nervous glance at her mother.

Lucy had just gotten her mother into bed with a cup of tea when she noticed a cable had been slipped under the front door. It was from Aunt Prissy.

INQUIRIES HAVE BEEN MADE STOP CERTAIN PARTIES SEEM MISINFORMED ABOUT OUR CONNECTION STOP KINDLY CORRECT AS SOON AS POSSIBLE STOP NOT CONVENIENT STOP

It was signed Priscilla Bancroft Devries. That was perhaps the cruelest blow of all.

"AN UNCOMMON YOUNG
WOMAN"

LUCY'S FIRST THOUGHT was that she could not show this to her mother. But then she realized that the cable had already been unsealed, and it was rather wrinkled. It must have already been torn open, read, and thrown on the floor in a fit of rage. Her father! But where was he?

She folded the cable and went outside, walking toward the cliffs where she had told Gus to wait.

His back was to her. The wind ruffled his thick black hair. She didn't mean to startle him, but he flinched as she slipped the cable in front of him.

"Do you know about this?" she asked.

He read it and then looked up.

"Not this cable specifically," he replied. There was almost a tortured sound in his voice.

"What are you talking about?"

"The word has gone out. The gossip machine has started."

"What word? What gossip machine?"

"You didn't notice Mrs. Van Wyck? The cut?"

"The cut?" It was as if Gus were speaking another language.

"She walked by your mother, ignoring her entirely. Everyone saw it. Cornelia Van Wyck is an expert at delivering these social torpedoes. She is a lethal weapon."

"I noticed that Mother suddenly seemed very pale and quite agitated, but then Percy Wilgrew came up, and . . . oh, I can't begin to tell you what he did."

"Percy? What did he do? Although there is nothing I would put beneath him. He's an utter cad."

Lucy turned bright red to the roots of her hair. There was no way she could tell him about the pearl from her combis. She cast her eyes down. "He obviously followed me and Phineas one afternoon. We were alone, unchaperoned." She laughed as she said the last word.

"And you were doing what . . . unchaperoned people in love might do."

"Just kissing." Lucy sobbed and buried her face in her hands.

"Oh, Lucy!" Gus sighed and touched her elbow lightly.

"I don't understand any of it."

Gus's face had grown hard. "It's what I hate about this whole stupid little world. Anna and I are going to escape it. I swear, if I have to give up every penny of my inheritance. Despite all the money, it is the most morally bankrupt existence imaginable. A native from the bush of Africa has more morals in the tip of his little finger than this bunch of louts!"

Gus Bellamy was fuming. But Lucy was still confused and felt she could not indulge him in his rant a moment longer. She needed to know things, facts. What was happening to her family?

"Sit down now. Right here on the ground and explain everything to me."

He looked at her, suddenly abashed. "I'm sorry. I was thinking about myself and not you." He took the cable and thwacked his hand with it. "This cable is most likely the result of certain inquiries that were probably initiated by Percy Wilgrew, the Duke of Crompton."

"Yes, go on."

"He apparently had been led to believe that you were the heiress to a substantial fortune with no entailments." Lucy groaned. It was becoming all too clear. "He found out otherwise and then, as we can assume, saw you and Phineas alone, which most likely spread fuel on the fire — although those rumors have not started to circulate yet. He began saying that you, your family were . . . sailing under false colors in order to fetch you a title."

"A title! As if being called a duchess would make up for that slimy, revolting man."

"To you, he is slimy and revolting, but he is considered the most amusing man on two continents. Charming, witty, an endless source of entertainment for bored rich people — particularly ladies. He hardly pays for a thing; since he is so fashionable he is a walking advertisement for the best wines, the best tailors. You notice the cravats in the pastel colors he has been wearing?"

"Not really," Lucy admitted, but she recalled her brief visit with Mrs. Van Wyck and how she had gone on about the duke's sense of style, his joie de vivre.

"Well, a dozen or more men here are wearing them now. My mother ordered a half dozen for both my father and me." Gus paused. "He has charmed them, enchanted them as much as any sorcerer. And so they will listen to anything he has to say. And right now, because of the rumors he has started, my father and the other church elders are meeting with your father at Bellemere."

"At Bellemere? Now?"

"Yes."

"Oh, poor Father. Are they going to fire him?"

"No. They'll let him finish the season."

"Finish the season but not be invited back." Lucy sighed. "And obviously no chance for the office of bishop of New York."

"No chance. The Van Wycks will definitely see to that. Sterling Van Wyck is the most powerful man in the diocese of New York."

Lucy was quiet for some time. Finally, she looked up at Gus. "Do you have any suggestions?"

"For what?"

"For anything?'

Gus looked at her steadily. "This, I know, is easier for me to say since I am a man and you are a young woman. But I would offer this."

"What?"

"Do what I'm going to do and live your own life, Lucy."

"Thank you, Gus, but . . ."

"But what?"

"It's not that much harder — at least not in some ways," she said quietly.

"You mean because you are a young woman, it is not that much harder?" He seemed confused.

"Yes, that is exactly what I mean." Lucy lifted her chin a bit as she spoke. *But not in the way you might imagine*, she thought.

"Well, I do think you are an uncommon young woman — so perhaps."

Lucy sighed. *More uncommon than you might ever believe.*

A MOTHER DECIDES

MARJORIE SNOW STOOD on the porch of the cottage and stared out at the windless iron gray sea. The thick clouds had sucked every bit of reflected light from the water so that the ocean looked like the gruel served in the poorhouses where she was obliged as a reverend's wife to volunteer one day a week.

The black spruce and pines felt as if they were closing in around her. The desolation, the grimness of this place seemed to augur the bleak future she, her husband, and Lucy now faced. And now she had jeopardized her oldest friendship. She could not bear to think about Prissy, but was it any easier to think about Lucy? How had she been so deceived by her own daughter? And Phineas Heanssler. How could Lucy be in love with this ordinary man?

The reverend, thinking he had heard the worst when he came back from the meeting of the church elders, had walked into an incomprehensible scene. The cottage seemed caught in a paroxysm of shrieking voices. As he entered, Marjorie wheeled around. She was screaming about a pink pearl button. Lucy was standing absolutely rigid with rage, shouting, "He is every bit a gentleman. How dare you?"

It took a full three minutes for the story to come out. And as the denouement, the pink button, assumed its place in the context of this sorry tale, the color drained from the reverend's face.

Lucy retreated to her bedroom. Marjorie, however, was not ready for sleep or the sleeping draft she would normally take when she was upset. She decided that her head must be crystal clear. The fog outside was bad enough; she refused to let it seep into her mind. As she stood on the porch of the cottage, gazing at the thickening fog, she told herself, "I must save what I can." And what she felt she could save was her daughter's reputation. So far, Percy Wilgrew had not breathed a word of the encounter between Lucy and Phineas in the woods. But there was no telling how long his silence would last. And that was just the problem. He might demand money from her. She would be lucky if Prissy ever spoke to her again, though Prissy did love Lucy. She could be convinced to lend some money if it could ensure his silence. *But there never really is insurance, is there?* Marjorie Snow reflected. This might go on for years and years. And why should Prissy, her oldest, dearest friend in the world, be subjected to that? Never. *He must be stopped.*

DEATH INCONVENIENT

"I'M GOING TO DO the violets and rosemary bouquet in the popover basket for the duke," Dolly Beal said as she arranged the tea tray with the jam pots and the china teapot.

"It's his last day?" Murla Jean Eaton asked.

"Yes," sighed Dolly.

"You going to miss him, girl, ain't you?" Edna Weed, the cook, said as she brought the freshly baked popovers from the oven to the counter where the tea trays were prepared for serving.

"It ain't like I'm in love or anything. It's just like . . . well . . . you know . . . it's sort of like going to a foreign land when he comes in. I mean, I know he ain't our kind."

"And we sure ain't his kind!" Murla Jean laughed.

"'Course we ain't. But it's like something different."

"You mean he don't smell like bait," Edna Weed said, giving the popover pan a delicate shake to loosen inflated buns that rose lofty and golden. Quickly she dropped them into the waiting baskets. "Scat! Before they fall!" she ordered.

No, he sure don't smell like bait, Dolly thought as she navigated through the tables draped in flowered cloths toward where the Duke of Crompton was holding forth with his usual companions, Mrs. Van Wyck, Mrs. Forbes, and Mrs. Bannister. The overhead fans turned languidly in the thick heat of August, and the women stirred the air with their hand fans as if it were a heavy batter.

"The Harvest Ball — always the last week in August. Mrs. Vanderbilt truly needs me to help with the arrangements. You know, the Russian crown prince is expected as well as the Marquis de Falaise. . . . Oh, Dolly! I was hoping you'd be on today. It's my last day."

"Yes, Your Grace. I know."

The ladies at the table exchanged meaningful glances. The first time Dolly served the duke, she had addressed him as Mr. Duke. Mrs. Van Wyck had taken her aside and explained that "Duke" was not his last name but a title and that she should simply address him as "sir," which she had done thereafter until this particular day. They conjectured that she must have gotten hold of a book of peerage and realized that to address him as "Your Grace" was, in fact, most proper. The ladies themselves being comparatively untutored in receiving titled English aristocrats, unlike their counterparts in Newport, had learned this form of address only a bit into the season and felt that "sir" would certainly suffice for Dolly.

"We'll miss you, Your Grace. We always make a little bouquet on folks' last day."

"Ah, violets! How lovely."

"And sprigs of rosemary — for remembrance so you won't forget us downeast here on this island."

"Forget? Never, Dolly! I have carefully packed away the recipe you so thoughtfully wrote out for the popovers."

"Well, enjoy, as I 'spect these still might be your last for a spell. They don't serve them down in Newport."

Mrs. Van Wyck shot Dolly a somewhat severe glance. This had to be one of the longer dialogues between a waitress and a guest; in Newport, rarely more than a single word was exchanged between staff and guests. Dolly blushed and gave a quick curtsy, then moved on to tend to her other two tables.

Returning to the kitchen, Dolly gave Lil, Edna Weed's assistant, the orders. "The Greens want their chamomile tea as usual. One order of popovers for the Whiteheads, with a small basket of blueberry muffins. No butter plate, please."

"Poor Mr. Whitehead. She don't let him eat a thing, do she? A tyrant that one," Lil said.

Suddenly, there was a commotion on the other side of the swinging doors.

"Sweet Jesus! Did Sally drop another tray?" Edna Weed exclaimed.

A small, frantic young woman, her starched cap askew, streaked into the kitchen. "Quick! Quick! Send someone for Doctor Holmes."

"Did you drop a tray?" Edna Weed shrieked.

"No, I did *not* drop a tray!" Sally shot back, her mild gray eyes suddenly fierce. "The duke has fainted. Collapsed."

"What?" Dolly gasped.

"Fell off his chair, gagging. Oh, you should see him. Sick as a dog, no worse. Face all twisted up like a halibut."

Dolly, who had been helping Edna shake loose the next batch of popovers, dropped the pan. The lofty bronze peaks quivered slightly, then folded in on themselves as she rushed through the swinging doors.

"Stand back! Stand back!" Mr. Haskell, the Abenaki Club's manager, ordered as he knelt beside the duke, who was crumpled on the floor, grunting in agony. His eyes had rolled back in his head, and his knees were drawn up to his chest. Then there was a terrible sound. Dolly was shocked when she realized it was the duke's own breath being torn from him like shreds of canvas sails split in a gale. These sounds were followed by a torturous inhalation and then nothing.

"The doctor's here!" someone cried out.

But it was too late. They all knew that as Dr. Lucius Holmes knelt by the stricken form. The doctor picked up the duke's wrist. His face was grim. He dropped the limp hand and tore open the duke's vest and shirt. Putting one hand over the other, he leaned hard on the chest and pressed.

His chest? Dolly thought. *The duke's chest? His Grace's chest? The body.* At some point, the Duke of Crompton had become in Dolly's mind merely a body. She turned away, tears in her eyes.

An offshore breeze stirred the floral tablecloths and on it a spirit glided past them, wafted away and blown back across the sea — to that foreign country England. As the spirit brushed by, Dolly, who had never left this Maine island, felt inclined to say, "Good-bye, godspeed, Your Grace," for during this brief summer, she had traveled miles and miles and miles, gone farther from this island than anyone could ever imagine.

❧   ❧   ❧

"I warn't in love with him, Dicky," she told her boyfriend later that evening. "I wouldn't never love anyone but you. And it's hard to explain, but it's just like when I was serving him tea and popovers . . ." She struggled to find the right words. "It was just like I'd seen a place I'd only heard about. I mean a whole 'nother continent. England!"

"But, Dolly, England ain't really a continent. If you look at it on the map. It ain't much bigger than an island, really."

Dolly was quiet for a while. "Maybe you're right, Dicky." She sighed. She could smell the scent of the bait. He'd been fishing with alewives, and though she knew he bathed, alewives stank to high heaven. Nevertheless, it was the fisherman's favorite bait at this time of year. "Maybe it is just an island, a really big one, but it's all the way across the Atlantic Ocean, and I just felt like I'd been there. Understand?"

Dicky Wedge did not really understand, but he loved Dolly and wanted to comfort her as best he could. "Well, Dolly, my girl, I'm glad you could be right here on Mount Desert Island with me and travel in that pretty head of yours all the way to England. And even if it's just an island, you're right; it is a country with a queen and princes. It's a shame about the way he died, though. Terribly painful. Worst kind of death."

"What do you mean, Dicky?"

"Well, they say it was poison — rat poison or something."

A FLASH IN THE NIGHT

IT WAS DONE. They could return to New York. The little contretemps with Prissy could be smoothed over, given time. The dream of Stephen becoming bishop would have to be set aside. *Set aside*, Marjorie thought. She liked those two words. There was the tincture of hope about them when linked together. She could still hope, just a bit. She was sure that if she could just get Lucy away from this island, she would forget that ridiculous boy.

It was well past midnight, but Marjorie could not sleep. There was no breeze, and the night was unusually warm. A mosquito had slipped into their bedroom, and its persistent droning had driven her from the bed. She put on a wrapper and walked out onto the porch. The water, untouched by wind, stretched like a dark enameled sea. A nearly full moon poured a path of silver almost directly to the beach below the cliff.

Lucy had spent so much time at the top of those cliffs, painting the view. Her daughter's watercolors were really exceptional. Perhaps they should consider having her take some lessons. There must be some place where she could be taught that would not ... not ... not be so full of artists! Lucy might even become a teacher herself for some well-off family. Then, for some unexplainable reason, Marjorie was taken with the notion of walking down from the porch, which she had not done all summer, for a better view of the scenes Lucy had painted.

She stood with her hand resting on the slender trunk of a birch tree and peered out at the sea. Clouds brushed across the moon, temporarily dappling the gleaming path of its light, but she spotted something flash where the silver had been. Something that appeared like a glittering rainbow bursting from the sea.

"What in the world!" she murmured and dared creep closer to the edge. The water near where she had seen the flash seemed to radiate with a dazzling array of colors. Something was swimming toward the beach, but she could not tell what it was. There was glitter beneath the surface, and a palpable energy emanated from the water. She felt it approaching, and a deep fear rose in her, but she was as rooted to the spot as the birch trees that surrounded her. A head broke through the surface. Sleek with water but a familiar shape. Though the hair was wet and dark, a sudden blast of moonlight ignited it like flames as she swam into the path of silver. "Lucy!" Marjorie Snow staggered slightly. *Work of the devil? A change-ling!* Lucy dove, and the magnificent tail lifted into the night. *No, not my daughter. Never was. Never will be.*

Concerning the death of the Duke of Crompton. Look to a young lady spurned in her love who sought vengeance and

*most likely will follow the duke to eter-
nity by taking the poison herself.*

Neville Haskell, the longtime manager of the Abenaki Club, for a third time read the note he had found slipped under his door. "What the devil!" He stared at the telephone on his desk, one of the few on the island. He had cursed the day it was installed and looked at it now as one might regard a caged animal. It rang so incessantly between eleven and one o'clock in the afternoon with bookings for tea that he actually would evacuate his office and have Miss Goodfellow sit at his desk and take the reservations. But now he picked it up and pressed the lever rapidly.

"Molly!" he rasped into the receiver.

"Yes, Mr. Haskell," Molly Whelan, the town's operator answered.

"Connect me to Constable Bundles."

"Homer?"

"Ayuh, he's the only constable I know on Mount Desert."

"Certainly."

There were a series of bleatings in his ear.

"Constable Bundles heah," the thick Maine accent honked through the receiver.

"Homer, it's Neville down at the Abenaki. You still working on that murder?"

"'Course I am. Biggest thing ever happened on this island. Got a reporter coming up from the *Boston Globe*."

"Well, you better get over here. I got a lead for you."

THE FACE OF A SAVAGE

LEAVING. Never had the word been so ominous, but never before had she feared leaving a place. She felt as if she were about to be torn from everything that had any meaning for her. She was leaving Phineas, leaving her two sisters, leaving the sea.

Despite being lost in her own thoughts, Lucy could not help but notice that her mother seemed extremely nervous this morning and rather distracted. She kept glancing toward the door as they ate their breakfast.

"Do you want some more tea, Mother?"

Marjorie seemed to wince. "No, nothing."

Not "nothing, dear," not "nothing, Lucy." Lucy supposed that since the incident of the cursed pink pearl button, she was no better than a slattern in her mother's eyes. She wanted to say something reassuring. She wanted again to try and explain that Phineas Heanssler was a decent, honest, hardworking young man. But she knew it was futile.

Lucy had hoped to see Muffy. She had wanted to tell her that it might be best if she did not serve as her bridesmaid. She was fairly sure that Mrs. Forbes would see to it that she did not but thought, for the sake of her own dignity, it was better for her to go and withdraw.

"Mother," Lucy began, but Marjorie still would not raise her eyes from her breakfast plate. "Mother," Lucy began again. "I have been thinking that perhaps it might be best if I called upon Muffy Forbes and offered to withdraw as her bridesmaid."

"Oh, Lucy dear," her father interjected, "I don't think that is necessary."

For the first time, Marjorie seemed to lift from the despondent vale that had enshrouded her all morning.

"Oh, Stephen, I feel it is very necessary. Most

appropriate." The muscle near her left eye began to flinch. There was a sharp rap on the door.

"I'll get it," Lucy said, eager for an excuse to leave the table.

"No, I will. Sit down!" Marjorie snapped.

Two uniformed men walked into the small dining room with Marjorie Snow.

"What's the meaning of this?" Reverend Snow stood up.

"Constable Bundles, sir." His words took on an odd life of their own. Lucy stood transfixed and yet was aware of every little detail, from the motes of dust circulating in a shaft of sunlight that fell on the breakfast table, to the cold metal as the constable's deputy fit the handcuffs around her wrist. She could see a distorted reflection of her own face spreading out across the polished surface of the cuffs and wondered if they shined them up just for her.

"Wait! Wait!" Her father was breathing heavily. "You say she poisoned the duke?"

"Innocent until proven guilty, Reverend. She is merely a suspect."

"A suspect!" the reverend roared.

Her father was a tower of rage, a foil for the absolute stillness of her mother, who stood like a figure carved from granite. Her eyes empty, oddly colorless, and staring at Lucy as if . . . *As if,* Lucy thought, and then it all came together for her, *as if I am a freak . . . a freak of nature. She saw me swimming.*

Lucy looked over at her mother as they led her toward the door.

"Take your shawl, dear." Her mother spoke mechanically. The word *dear* was as cold as the metal cuffs around her wrists. She could not reach for the shawl because of her bound wrists. Her father stepped over to the hook where her shawl and small, embroidered handbag hung. He removed first the bag and then the shawl.

"What's this?" The reverend looked down as a dusting of powder fell from the handbag.

"Don't touch it, Reverend," Constable Bundles barked.

"What is it?"

"Poison, possibly. Rat poison."

Lucy looked directly at her mother. "You did this!" she seethed. She caught a glint of cunning light in her mother's eyes. Marjorie Snow's face was immobile, void of visible expression, yet there was the barely discernible shadow of a bland malignancy. For lurking beneath the implacable mask was the face of a savage.

"THE POISONER"

"HEY, MISS SNOW, you made it into the *Ellsworth American* and the *Boston Globe* — all the way to Boston, how about that! You're putting us on the map, de-ah." Mr. Greenlaw, the prison guard, sat in a room next to where his only prisoner was incarcerated.

Lucy was unsure how long she had been in the jail in Thomaston, Maine. It could have been just a few days, a week, a month. What did it really matter? She had quickly learned to close her ears to his seemingly continuous narration. She stopped listening when he had tried to recall when the last hanging in the county had occurred — was it '70 or '71? He was fairly sure it was when his father had been the guard.

"You don't mind, do you, if I bring my grandson by to meet you?" he had asked one day. Lucy had said nothing, and he had obviously taken her silence as acquiescence. So a short time after this latest news bulletin, she was surprised to hear a child's voice coming down the corridor and the light skipping of his feet on the stone floor. The two sounds were so incongruous to the setting that she was immediately alert. Soon a little face was pressing against the bars. "That her, Grandpa?"

"That's her, Joey. That's Lucy Snow. The poisoner."

"Can you get her to come closer?" the child asked.

"Miss Lucy, would you be kind enough to walk a bit closer? My grandson Joey here, he ain't really ever seen anybody in the cell 'cept for the town drunks. Would you kindly walk up to the bars and make a little boy happy?"

Kindly, Lucy thought. Why would the man bother with such a word? But she rose from the stool and walked a few steps toward the bars.

"Look at that, Grandpa, look at those sparkly things floatin' round her feet."

Until that moment, Lucy had not realized that her skin felt different. She was suddenly overcome by a fierce itching and a feverish heat. She stopped and looked at her hands. They appeared red. She remembered Hannah's story about being put on an orphan train that took her far from Boston, far from the sea to the middle of the country — Kansas. Her skin had seemed to dry out to the point where she was shedding what she later realized were scales. Lucy stopped walking.

"I am feeling quite feverish. Perhaps I should not come any closer. I wouldn't want to infect the child."

CLERGYMAN'S DAUGHTER SUSPECT
IN DUKE'S MURDER

On Tuesday, Lucy Snow, the daughter of prominent New York clergyman Stephen Snow, was arrested for the murder of English aristocrat Percy Wilgrew, the Duke of Crompton. On August 15, Mr. Wilgrew collapsed at the exclusive Abenaki Club in

Bar Harbor, Maine. According to medical examiners, the cause of death was due to ingesting rat poison. Officials say an anonymous note delivered to the Abenaki Club manager, Mr. Neville Haskell, led to the arrest of Miss Snow. According to sources who requested to remain anonymous, Miss Snow had been recently jilted by the duke.

Hannah slammed down the *Boston Globe* on the counter. "She didn't love him. She was not *jilted* by him."

"Now, Hannah, how would you ever know?" Mrs. Bletchley, the cook at Gladrock, said as she beat the batter for the blueberry muffins.

Hannah had said too much. She had to think fast. "I — I saw them at the Fourth of July party here. I could just tell that she didn't like him, but he was pursuing her — madly."

"Well, maybe she got fed up," Mrs. Bletchley offered, "and decided to do him in. Poison. Imagine that! However did she get the poison into those jam pots over at the Abenaki?"

"Exactly! How?" Hannah stood up. Her cheeks were flaming.

Mrs. Bletchley looked at her with alarm.

"Hannah dear. You're quite upset. Perhaps you want to take the afternoon off. No one's coming for luncheon today. I'm sure Mr. Marston wouldn't mind."

"What wouldn't I mind?" Mr. Marston, the Hawleys' butler, walked into the kitchen.

"Hannah's feeling a bit out of sorts. This murder and all."

"Oh, yes, terrible thing. Makes one rather nervous, doesn't it? Imagine having to check your jam pot every time you want a popover. I understand the Abenaki is closing for the summer. No, Hannah, I wouldn't mind. Take the afternoon off."

"Thank you, sir." Hannah curtsied and left the kitchen.

She had to get in touch with May. They had been meeting almost every night since Lucy's arrest. But it wasn't night now; it was broad daylight. She couldn't exactly swim out to Egg Rock Island and appear at May's door at the lighthouse. What would May's father say? She heard Ettie out on the porch, arguing with Miss Ardmore, her governess. "Why do I have to sit here on a beautiful day and learn irregular French verbs. It's a crime!"

"Now, Ettie. We've had enough real crimes on this island. So please, dear, don't be hyperbolic."

"I don't believe for one minute that Lucy Snow murdered that stupid duke."

Hannah froze in her tracks. The intensity in Ettie's voice cut like a hot blade through the air. She walked out onto the porch.

"Miss Ardmore, forgive me for interrupting Ettie's lessons. But those hair ribbons that you were so certain you had lost forever and ever, Ettie — guess where I found them."

What hair ribbons? Ettie thought. Her brow crinkled. It suddenly dawned on her that Hannah had heard what she'd just said about Lucy. The hair ribbons were a complete ruse.

"Please, Miss Ardmore, let me take Ettie for just a

minute so I can show her exactly where they were and how silly she is not to have seen them. They would have bitten her on the nose."

"Of course. I think perhaps we should give up for now on the irregular verbs."

As soon as they were in Ettie's bedroom and Hannah had shut the door, Ettie blurted out, "Hair ribbons? Now really, Hannah, what is this all about?"

"It's about my sisters," Hannah said. Tears quivered in her eyes, turning them into huge green pools. Hannah fell to her knees and embraced the small girl. "Ettie, we need your help. You must come with me to meet May, my other sister. May Plum, the lighthouse keeper's daughter."

"I'll do anything, Hannah. Anything to help you. To help Lucy. We'll think of something, somehow."

"I can trust you. I can trust May." And she thought to herself she could trust Phineas Heanssler.

"Can you trust Stannish Whitman Wheeler?"

Hannah was taken aback by Ettie's question. "So you know about us?"

Ettie avoided her eyes. "I just . . . I just had a suspicion, back when we had to pose for the portrait. I saw how he looked at you. Can you trust him?"

"I'm not sure, Ettie."

"He's one of you, isn't he?"

Hannah was shocked. "How did you ever know?"

"I'm not sure. Maybe it was his eyes — the green. There was just something about him that made me feel that he was . . . was . . ."

"Mer," Hannah said softly.

"Yes, mer," Ettie replied.

"He was. However, he's made his choice. But right now you need to meet my sister."

Ettie felt a deep thrill course through her. "Will we swim?"

"No, dear. We'll take the mail boat and walk right in through the front door of the lighthouse."

EPILOGUE

EDGAR PLUM WAS SITTING at the table when he heard the knock on the door. He walked over to open it. *My goodness*, he thought. *The spittin' image of May.* But who was this little girl with her? Looked as if she was one of the summer people's kids all decked out in her little sailor dress and fancy kid-leather boots. Little straw hat with a ribbon band perched on her head pert as a bird.

"Hello, miss." He sighed. *Might as well admit it*, he thought. *No use beating around the bush.* "Been expectin' you."

"You have, sir?"

"Call me Gar, de-ah, for I feel as if I'm at least your uncle."

May appeared on the staircase, her eyes red from crying. Hannah looked up at her. "He knows?"

"He knows everything."

"Come in, de-ah." He wrapped his long arms around her. "Been a long time coming, hasn't it?" he whispered into her hair and patted her back. "Now who's your young friend here?"

"I'm Henrietta Grace Hawley. And I know everything, too, and yes, Mr. Plum, it's been a long time coming."